D1524269

Love Like Her

USA TODAY BESTSELLING AUTHOR
CLAUDIA BURGOA

Sign up for my newsletter *to receive updates about upcoming books and exclusive excerpts.*

www.claudiayburgoa.com

For Ana Patiño. Gracias.
Thank you for everything. For being the inspiration to some of the best mom's I've written. For teaching me to believe in myself. You'll be missed but forever loved.

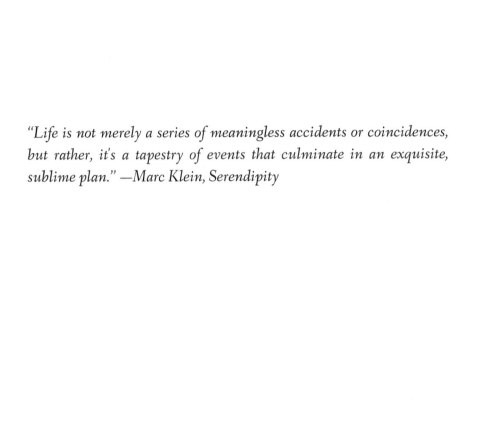

"Life is not merely a series of meaningless accidents or coincidences, but rather, it's a tapestry of events that culminate in an exquisite, sublime plan." —Marc Klein, Serendipity

Chapter One

Olivia

WE DON'T MEET people by accident. Every relationship we have has a cause.

Mom always says people come into our lives to teach us a lesson, to learn from us, or to love. Love isn't necessarily romantic love, though.

It's love of your friends, coworkers, and, well, yes, lovers.

Some people stay for a season. Others might remain for a lifetime. Nurturing relationships can be daunting when people come and go in your life like a revolving door.

But see, the nature of life is constant change.

It's ironic when we, as humans, are social by nature. We seek company, comfort, and security from each other. We all want to be loved and to have a sense of permanency.

To be loved by our parents, our families, our friends, but the one love we all seek is the romantic, head over heels, I can't live without my soulmate kind of love.

Are soulmates real? Some swear by them. Others are still alone, searching the four corners of the world for something that might be a fantasy. Do I believe in them? I do, but I'm certainly not looking for anyone. I'm way too young to even think about a serious relationship. At some point, I hope to have what Dad does and be less like Mom.

Mom doesn't believe in love or soulmates. She's practical—or maybe cynical.

She says you love; you release them when your time is over, and you move on to the next person. Dad swears there's one person for you. Of course he does. He's been with his husband since I was seven. I love Dan as a second father, but my parents' divorce and their relationship kind of ruined my life.

I sound selfish, but I'm not. Their custody agreement has been daunting for me.

After the divorce, Mom moved back to Canada, where she's from. Since it was the middle of the school year, I stayed with Dad and Dan. The next school year, I moved with Mom. That should've been the end of it. Olivia stays with her mother. She sees her father every other holiday and lives bitterly ever after.

Things are never that easy when it comes to my life. Since then, I have moved between countries every other year. I'm not kidding here. They decided it'd be best for me to be with them one full year at a time.

If a psychologist got a hold of me, they'd have a field day. I'm sure they could write a paper or even a book called *Child from an Amicable Nonsense Divorce*. If my parents had had a typical divorce and custody agreement, I wouldn't be stranded in JFK, begging Dad to pay for a hotel room.

"You made your choice, Olivia Evelyn. You should've been here yesterday."

Ouch, he's throwing the middle name.

"My last final was earlier today. I couldn't just skip it because my dad thought it'd be best if I made it home by Sunday," I remind him, keeping my voice under control. He is infuriating. I'm not in charge of my school's schedule.

"Well, I don't understand why you flew to New York instead of Toronto."

To save three hundred dollars, I don't answer. I used the money to buy him and Dan their Christmas presents. And I bought a cute pair of boots I found on sale.

"I like to be thrifty, Dad," I defend myself. "Going through New York seemed like a good idea."

"What did you say last summer?" he pauses, "Right, you're an adult. I should respect your decisions. Well, as an adult, figure out what you're going to do."

"You want me to loiter around the airport like that Tom Hanks movie? Let me remind you that this is real life. The stores and restaurants aren't even open. Do you want me to starve?"

Okay, I'm laying it thick on the drama, but he's being unreasonable.

"Liv, I love you, but this was your decision, not mine. You're going to have to figure out what to do for the next day."

"Couple of days," I correct him. "They didn't find any seats for me until Wednesday."

"There aren't any rooms available in any hotel. Even the suites are booked," I hear Dan's voice. "Can we do anything else?"

"I told you we weren't paying for a room, Danny boy," Dad says.

"We can't leave her stranded," Dan, who is the voice of reason between the two, argues.

"Well, you just said it. There aren't any rooms available."

"Fine, I'll die of hypothermia," I claim. It's time to pull the ultimate weapon: Guilt trip. "Just remember this is on you. I want to make sure you write on my grave, 'Olivia Evelyn Sierra. Loving daughter. Wannabe astronaut. She never grew up to save the world. She died of hypothermia because she wanted to be an adult.'"

I hear a snort close by. When I turn, a guy is staring at me, amused at something I said, or just laughing at me because I might have something on my face. Who knows at this rate? It's been a long Monday. My only hope is that I didn't flunk my test or I'm doomed.

"Leave the dramatics to your mother," Dad states.

I move my focus from tall, hot, dark, and yummy to my conversation. Guys like him are not part of my menu. I haven't graduated from happy meals yet. Ugh, I need to stop speaking in Holly's lingo. I sound like her and her latest trend. She compares men with food. According to her, fooling around is a happy meal. Eating an entrée is going all the way with a guy.

"Liv, it's too close to Christmas, and there aren't any rooms available in the area. I could search in New Jersey, but I doubt you'll find a cab to take you there," Dan says.

"Hey, Dan," I greet him. "How upset is Dad?"

"The usual. He'll cool down by the time you're home, sweetheart," he assures me. "I'll transfer some money to your debit card. If I find a hotel room, I'll call you. Stay at the airport."

"Thank you, Dan," I say, chastising myself because I forgot my phone charger in the car.

"Call if you need me. Please, don't be reckless."

"I'm a daredevil," I joke.

"You're not," he states. "But sometimes you don't think about the consequences—like your father."

When Mom says I'm a lot like my father, I'm not sure if she does it to insult me, complain about my personality, or remind me he's despicable. He's not. After so many years, I've learned to differentiate between her spiteful remarks and reality. When Dan says it, it's just a statement. He doesn't say it to hurt me. I also know he adores Dad. So, even if I do stuff that he doesn't approve of, I amuse him and he loves me.

"Love you, Dan," I say before hanging up.

"Love you too, Livy girl."

I wish I could call Mom and ask her to bail me out of this one. She won't.

My parents are upset because I changed their schedule. They prefer not to split holidays, summers, or birthdays. Unfortunately for them, I'm an adult. Their custody agreement doesn't apply anymore. Fortunately for me, I can go wherever I want.

My phone rings, and it's Holly, my best friend.

"Hi."

"Hey, girl," she squeals. I move the phone away from my ear.

"You seem to be excited."

"My bestie is almost home."

Holly and I have been friends since we were in preschool. Her family lived right across the street from us. When my parents divorced, Dad and Dan made sure I stayed in touch with Holly and a few other friends from the neighborhood. Out of all my friends, Holly is the one with whom I connect with the most.

"Or she won't be there until Wednesday." I sigh and tell her everything that's happened to me. The flat tire on my way to Halifax airport, the storm, and my father not paying for my hotel room.

"You want me to check if there are any hotels?"

"I only have two hundred dollars." I don't know how much money Dan is going to add to my account, but I'd rather not misuse it. What if I have a real emergency? "The only hotel I could afford is one of those where they give you a brick for a pillow and a bat to kill the roaches."

Again, the guy close by laughs. I itch to reach for my camera and snap a picture of him.

He's dreamily handsome. He's tall with dark, sexy, unruly hair. His dark scruffy jaw makes him look older, but his big dark melted chocolate eyes tell a different story. He's young. The guy is probably in college. He has a boyish smile and a dimple in his left cheek.

A shiver runs up and down my spine when his eyes sweep my body from head to toe and winks at me.

Melting.

He's so hot.

"Do I amuse you?"

He smirks and winks. "You're entertaining."

"Who is that?"

"Some guy who is listening to my conversation," I respond.

"Is he hot?"

"You have no idea."

"Take a picture of him," Holly requests.

"At the moment, I'm busy trying to figure out how not to die of hypothermia, hunger, or being kidnapped by a yeti."

"That's part of the Himalayan folklore," the hot guy butts into my conversation. "If he even existed, he wouldn't catch a plane just to come and attack you."

I glare at him. "Thank you, Wikipedia, for your useful information."

"Just trying to save you from your wild imagination." He pretends to tip an imaginary hat.

Holly laughs. "He sounds pretty hot and funny."

"If you're into that kind of thing," I pretend to be unamused, but if I weren't in the middle of an existential crisis, I'd be all over the guy.

He's a hot, funny college guy. We don't have many of those in Kemptown, Nova Scotia. Okay, now I'm exaggerating. There are hot college guys, but they don't notice me.

"So, when do I see you?" Holly asks.

"Wednesday," I confirm. "Maybe you can pick me up because Dad isn't happy with me."

"The man adores you. I'm sure he already forgave you."

"Or not."

"Call me if you need me."

"I don't have much battery. You might not hear from me until I land," I say and hang up.

The hot guy is still looking at me. "Why are you here?" I ask him. Although, I wanted to start with something like, "Are you a serial killer of sorts?"

He smirks. "Obviously, I like to visit airports to watch people when I'm bored."

"I bet it is better than cable."

He shoves his hands in his pockets and nods. "A lot better than *The Amazing Race*," he concludes.

"I love that show," I claim excitedly. "Can you imagine traveling from country to country to those places only the locals know about and finding clues?"

He shakes his head. "It's not that great."

"Were you a contestant?"

"No. I traveled with my parents around the world," he states.

I look around. "Where are your parents?"

"They live in Colorado," he answers. "I was on my way to visit them, but..."

"Stranded, huh?"

"Indeed. I heard you don't have any place to go."

"Eavesdropping much?" I arch an eyebrow and give him a judging glare.

"Let's just say *you* don't know the meaning of inside voice," he explains. "So, did they kick you out of the dorm?"

I frown. "They didn't kick me—Oh," I pause and clear my throat instead of laugh. "I go to school in Canada. Instead of flying through Toronto, I came to New York. Not the brightest decision, I just won't admit it. How about you?"

"Listen, I know this is a weird offer, but if one of my sisters was in your position, I hope someone would offer them a place where they can stay. Would you like to come to my apartment?"

"Ha!" I stare at my phone that's almost out of battery. "Is this the part where the gullible foreigner says yes, and you lock me in some weird warehouse?"

He laughs. "Then your epitaph will read, 'Olivia Evelyn. Died by the hands of the airport killer.'"

"You forgot to add, 'Loving daughter. Wannabe astronaut. She died a virgin by the hands of'"—I look at him—"'The Hottie Killer.' After they apprehend you, the headlines will read something like: He lured his victims with acts of kindness. They'll catch you when you try to kill your fourteenth victim."

"Why is that?" He crosses his arms, and one hand goes to his chin. He scratches it and says, "I'm smart enough to know how to lure you, how to dispose of the bodies, and look like a good guy. Where did I go wrong?"

"Well, for one, fourteen is my lucky number," I inform him. "By then, the FBI will realize that witty, five foot four young females with reddish-brown hair are disappearing in the city of New York."

I point at the CCTV camera. "There's a video of the first girl who disappeared around Christmas time. They'll recognize your face. Boom, I help solve the crime from beyond the grave."

He is hugging himself and laughing. "Am I able to escape? Do they kill me? I need to know what happens to me."

"You get a life sentence without the possibility of parole. Dad will fight to have you pay for all your crimes. He'll make sure that your jail cell has posters of my face, so you're reminded of why you ended up in jail. That's when my family will finally learn what happened to me. They'll realize that by not paying for a fancy hotel room, I was left in the hands of some psychotic man."

"Psychopath," he corrects me.

"Well, you would know."

"You do know there are too many holes in that theory?"

I shrug one shoulder. "Probably. If you don't like it, you can make up your own story."

He extends his hand. His head angles slightly so he can see me better. He's almost a foot taller than me. A frisson of energy runs through me. There's a glimmer of amusement in his captivating eyes. "Eros Brassard. It's nice to meet you, Olivia Evelyn."

That voice is so low and sexy. It makes every cell in my body vibrate. Something inside me knots my insides in different directions. My legs wobble. The way he says my name—his touch. I don't understand what exactly is holding me in place, unable to speak or snatch my hand back.

It takes me a couple of seconds to remind myself that I'm not like other girls. I don't gush around a hot guy. My life is already too complicated to add guys to it. Crushes are a major complication. Pulling my hand away from him, I grab my backpack, my carry-on bag, and I run to the nearest restroom.

Chapter Two

Eros

I HAVE TWO CHOICES: Go after Olivia Evelyn, who I clearly don't want to learn she died of something or another, or head home. As the oldest of my siblings, I'm always looking after my sisters. All three of them. Well, mostly Nyx and Persephone, who are only a couple of years younger than me. Calliope is nine years younger. We don't run in the same circles.

The point is that if any of them were stranded in the middle of a blizzard without a place to stay, I hope that someone would lend them a hand. I can't offer to pay for a hotel room if there are any available. My options are to remain in the airport with her until my flight takes off on Wednesday or bring her to my apartment.

My phone rings. It's Nyx. She's a couple of years younger than me, but sometimes she takes on the role of the oldest sister. I let her boss me around because it makes her happy.

"Nyx?"

"We're about to take off," she states. By we, I assume she's talking about her and Persy. They live in North Carolina. Nyx goes to Duke, while Persy goes to the University of North Carolina. The three of us have always done everything together—except college. I chose Columbia University.

"Call me when you get home," I request.

"I'm guessing they canceled your flight."

I sigh. "Yes. I won't be home until Wednesday."

"You're cutting it too close. I told you to leave on Sunday. Why don't you fly out tomorrow?"

"I got out of work at two today," I remind her. "Tomorrow's flights are all booked. The storm isn't tampering down until tomorrow night. I figured it was safer to book it for Wednesday morning. I should be at the parents' around two o'clock."

"Do you have food at home?"

"I'm prepared," I assure her. This isn't my first storm. "Let me ask you something."

"Shoot."

"If you're stuck at the airport with nowhere to go and a guy offers you a place to stay, would you think it's creepy?"

"Yep," she answers, mumbles something, and then says, "You tried to save the day, didn't you?"

"I can't just leave her stranded," I explain. "She went to hide in the restroom. We joked about me being a serial killer, but maybe she believes it."

"You're like a puppy. Harmless and a fool." She sighs. "How old is she?"

"Nineteen or twenty? She's about Persy's age."

"Why don't you stay with her at the airport."

"Or I can just leave her."

"What if it was Callie?"

"She's nothing like Callie." My sister is twelve and I can see her throwing a major tantrum in the middle of the airport. "She's actually kind of funny."

I don't add cute to the description. Olivia is beautiful. Mahogany colored hair, big hazel eyes that contrast with her tan skin, long eyelashes that frame her sparkling eyes. She's petite, curvy, and has a pretty smile. If I add more to her description, she's going to think I'm into her. Which I'm not. The only reason I'm offering her a place to stay is because she's stranded and doesn't have anywhere to go.

"Give her the phone," she orders.

"I told you, she's hiding in the restroom."

Nyx growls. "You already scared her. Go inside and yell, 'Guy coming in.' Make sure to close your eyes."

"I'm not doing that, Nyx Andromeda."

Getting close to the entrance, I yell, "Olivia, it's Eros. My sister would like to have a word with you."

"Your sister?" I hear her voice from somewhere inside the bathroom. "Is that another tactic to kidnap me?"

"No, I'm serious. My sister would like a word with you."

She walks outside the bathroom and glares at me, then at the phone. "Why would she want to talk to me?"

I shrug.

"Is she your partner? I thought psychopaths worked alone."

"We usually do, but at this time of the year it's easier with a helper. We learned it from Santa." I wink at her.

"That's not funny, Eros!" Nyx yells. "You can be so dense."

Olivia grins and takes the phone.

"Hi." She nods, shakes her head, and gives me a curious look. "I can see the resemblance. Well, my parents drilled the stranger danger motto at a young age. It's harder for serial killers like him to get me alone. Obviously, if you say he's safe, I should believe you. Because what are the chances that you are his accomplice."

Olivia presses her lips together. "I can do that. Thank you and have a nice flight."

She hands over my phone.

"What did she want?" I ask curiously.

"You know, the usual," she explains, waving her hand. "Call nine-one-one, kick him in the nuts, don't feed him after midnight or he turns into a monster."

"Nyx wouldn't say that," I claim.

She frowns. "I talked to Persephone."

"Huh?" I scratch my temple. "I was on the phone with Nyx."

"So, what's with the Greek mythology names?"

I grin. "My parents are fans. Our youngest sister is Calliope."

She nods a couple of times. "That's a lot better than Olivia Evelyn. My parents named me after my grandmothers. I adored the ladies, but I would've liked to have something a little more original and a lot less old lady."

"You don't know what you wish for. Try living with the name Eros Zephyrus," I argue.

She laughs. "That's—it's a joke, right?"

I shake my head. "Nope. My parents are... different. What did my sisters want?"

"Persephone said the puppy face is real. You wouldn't kill a fly or an insect—or you'll get in trouble with your parents."

"Persy talks fast. I'm sure there was more," I say, staring at her.

She shrugs one shoulder. "Maybe, and I can't tell you because it's a secret. It's the only way to stay alive until I have to board my plane to San Francisco."

"Are you having fun?"

"Slightly. I can't believe you had your sisters call me."

"It wasn't exactly like that. They called and I asked them what to do."

"Because you're afraid of the storm?"

"Honestly, it's unsettling to think of what could happen to you."

"The inside of the airport is safe," she mumbles.

"That movie, *The Terminal*, was fantasy. I prefer to know that you're safe. If I have to stay with you, that's fine." I tilt my head toward the waiting area. "Why don't we take a seat?"

She follows me, sits on a chair, and sets her luggage on each side of her seat. I guess I'm not allowed to sit next to her.

I take a seat across from her and pull out a couple of granola bars from my backpack and offer them to her. "Have you eaten?"

"Thank you," she takes both, places one inside her backpack, and opens the other one. "What is it like to have three sisters?"

"That's a strange question. Nyx and Persy are my best friends," I inform her. "We traveled with our parents to archeological sites. We were our only constant. Sometimes I played dolls with them. Other days, we would be climbing trees, throwing the ball, or we hung out with my parents."

"So that's why you traveled a lot? Your parents are archeologists?"

I nod and tell her more about our trips. The ones I remember the most, the food we ate, the languages we know, and the people we've met. She stops me to ask questions and hangs onto every word I tell her. As I relive the memories, it feels as if she's holding my hand and experiencing them with me.

"How about you? Any siblings?"

She shakes her head. "No. I'm an only child. My parents divorced when I was young."

"That sucks. I'm sorry."

"It's fine. They divorced years ago. If you think about it, divorce children are more typical than children from lengthy and happy marriages." She smiles. "I'm the norm. You're an almost extinct species."

"You like to tweak things around, don't you?"

She takes a bite of her granola bar and then looks at me. "It's a coping mechanism. Divorced parents, remember?"

"So, you're Canadian, but your Dad currently lives in San Francisco because..."

She narrows her eyes. "There you go again, trying to fetch information."

"I just told you my entire life, and you can't even answer a question?"

She taps her lip. "There wasn't a question. You're just implying." Her playful eyes stare at me. "I was born in San Francisco. Dad's from there too. Mom is Canadian. After the divorce, she moved back to Toronto." She yawns. "You don't want to know about them. It's boring, lengthy, and annoying."

My phone rings and I notice it's after ten. No wonder I'm hungry and tired.

"Hey," I greet Persy. "You guys made it to our parents'?"

"Yes. We just arrived. How's Olivia?"

I look at Olivia, who is yawning again and rubbing her eyes. "Tired."

"Offer her to go to your apartment now. She might be ready to trust you."

"I hope so because I'm falling asleep also." I yawn too.

"Your sisters?"

I nod in response.

"So, I don't have much in my fridge, but there's plenty of food for us to survive the storm," I offer.

She smiles. "I..."

"It's hard to trust someone you just met," I state and grab her hand, encasing it with both of my hands. "I'm taking the risk bringing you to my place. For all I know, you are a thief that takes advantage of gullible idiots who try to do the right thing."

She blinks a couple of times and releases a loud laugh. I'm getting used to her voice, her laugh, and that hunger to learn more and more. I wouldn't be surprised if she's one of those people who stays in school through her twenties.

"What do you say, Olivia?"

"Liv," she says. "My friends and family call me Liv."

"Does that make us friends?"

"Probably. I'd rather say I was at my friend Eros's house during the storm. It has a better ring than saying I went home with a stranger."

"By Wednesday we'll be best friends," I assure her, grabbing her hand.

I don't know why I did it. There's no way I can explain the sparks flying between us. I've never felt anything like this before. It's so strange and yet, it feels perfect. Fitting.

Is there such a thing as being compatible with a perfect stranger?

Chapter Three

Olivia

I HAVE no idea how we are going to make it to his house when everything is closed. Eros makes a couple of calls, and thirty minutes later an SUV is picking us up outside the airport.

"That was fast," he tells the driver.

"There's no one on the streets," the guy explains. "As soon as I heard they were canceling flights, I thought you'd be calling. You took your sweet little time."

Eros glances at me and smiles. "I had an issue that took longer to solve than I expected."

"Get in the car. The roads are getting pretty bad, so this might be a long drive."

"You have a driver?"

He shakes his head. "Not exactly."

It feels awkward to continue our conversation in the car. I don't know the guy who is taking us to Eros's place. It's past one in the morning when we arrive at his residence. I had no idea what to expect, but I open my eyes wide when I see the building.

"You live on Park Avenue?" I'm a little impressed at the sight of the limestone building. How rich is he? The entrance is covered with a small roof that has the building number. There's a doorman inside opening the door for us.

"Eros, ma'am," he greets us and nods.

"How's the family, Norm?"

"At home, like every New Yorker. I thought you were visiting your parents."

"The flight got canceled."

"I hope you can get there before Christmas day."

Eros smiles. "Everything is planned accordingly. I'm sure Mom's already pulling out the tarot cards to confirm that I'll be there. Or she'll find one of those figurines she collects. There has to be one she can chant to so it'll stop snowing."

Norm shakes his head. "Does your mom know that you mock her this much?"

"Sure, and I'm still her favorite," he claims.

"Have a good night, Eros."

"Same, Norm." He shakes the doorman's hand.

"Good night, sir." I wave and follow Eros toward the elevator.

I didn't peg the guy as some rich kid living in New York. He looks normal. When we enter his apartment, I understand this is his parents' home, assuming they're archeologists as he claims.

"Your parents' collection of artifacts?"

He shakes his head. "No, this is Gil's place."

"Who is Gil?"

"He's my godfather. I'm sort of subleasing it while I go to school. The car was his. The driver works for him. I use him when I have emergencies," he states.

I whistle. "You can afford to sublease this while going to school?"

"Fine. I pay for the utilities and keep the place tidy enough."

The apartment is prominent, like one of those residences used as a movie set. I always imagined that New Yorkers lived in tiny apartments. I guess it's all about perception and listening to people complain about their rooms being as big as a closet or not owning much furniture because their stuff doesn't fit.

"Where is Gil?" I ask, hoping that there's not another guy in this place.

He shrugs. "Somewhere around the world, digging while making a documentary," he states. "It's funny how before when I traveled with my parents, I practically saw him every day. Now that I'm in one place, his house of all places, I haven't seen him in two years. Unlike my parents, he continues working. His life is his work."

I look around, trying to find something that says this apartment belongs to Gil. It seems more like a cool museum where everything is out on display and available to the touch. Finally, when I get to what I assume is some sort of office, I find several pictures. There are a few of them with him and a boy. When Eros enters, I show him one of them and ask, "Is this his son?"

"No, that's me," he answers.

He scans the pictures and shows me another one of Gil with two girls that look a lot alike. They are about five or maybe six.

"These two monsters are my sisters," he explains.

"Nyx and Persy," I assume.

He nods. "Gil is part of our family. He is Dad's best friend. When I got accepted to Columbia, he offered to pay my tuition and to use his apartment. Unlike him, my parents don't have much. I accepted subleasing this place. My parents would be offended if he paid for my college, but they're fine if I live in his house for almost nothing."

This Gil guy looks so happy in all the pictures. I point at a man who looks a lot like Eros but a few years older. He's with Gil and Eros. "Your Dad?"

"Yep. Octavio Brassard."

"Does Gil have a family?"

"His parents died when he was in college," Eros explains. "He's relied on his friends all his life. We're his family."

"No wife, boyfriend... he's just alone?"

"Why do you sound so baffled about his relationship status?"

I shrug. "He sounds like an interesting person. I feel like he should have someone to be there for him. A person that will pack her things and travel with him to the end of the world."

"It feels weird that you're romanticizing his life," he states.

"Maybe it comes from living with a mother who keeps kissing toads in hopes of finding her temporary prince. She's not a fan of the soul mate theory," I explain. "A part of me wishes she'd find just one guy and settle in with him. Like Dad did."

"Why did your parents divorce?"

"Dad was in love with someone else," I answer the short version.

"People shouldn't marry just because it is logical. They should do it because it feels right," I say out loud. "You should be with the person you can't live without because they complete you in a way that no one else does."

"You sound pretty passionate about it," he states. "Why don't we go to the kitchen while you tell me more about this love theory? I'm starving."

"I could use some food."

The kitchen is not much different from the apartment. It's spacious, modern with earth tone tiles, state-of-the-art appliances, and dishes that could be dated to pre-colonial times.

Eros opens the stainless steel refrigerator. "Do you want anything to drink?"

"Water is fine," I say. "How can I help?"

"What would you like to eat?"

"I'd love a grilled cheese sandwich and chicken noodle soup," I say, hopeful.

He opens the door next to the stove, opens it, and pulls out a can. "Is this okay?"

"Perfect."

I'm grateful that he has all the ingredients to make my favorite comfort food. I take over the kitchen and start cooking. Once I'm done, I plate the sandwiches, serve the soup in a couple of bowls, and set the small kitchen table.

"This looks delicious," he says, setting a couple of water glasses next to our food. "Are grilled sandwiches your specialty," Eros asks.

I cock an eyebrow, wondering what he means. "You seemed so excited about preparing them."

The memory of learning how to make them draws a big smile on my face. "Dan taught me how to cook simple things when I was young. I guess it was a way to bond."

I take a bite of my sandwich.

"Who is Dan?"

After I chew and swallow my food, I answer, "Dad's husband."

"The reason why your parents divorced?"

"I'm the reason why Dad and Dan broke up and my parents had

to get married," I clarify. "My parents were in a loveless marriage because they were trying to do the right thing."

"It was their love for you," he states. "I assume they are happy now."

"I'm not sure about Mom, but Dad has been happy since he got back together with Dan," I respond, taking a spoonful of soup.

"So, I guess Dan has been trying to find ways to include himself in your life since he's not really your parent and you only visit them on holidays," he states.

That's a great theory, but it's not close to the truth.

"No. I lived with Dad every other year," I clarify. "But I guess you're right. Dan tried to be like the fun parent. He's always playing the reasonable one against Dad's strict rules—or Mom's nonsense."

I tell him how it was growing up with my family. It's hard for people to understand how I survived moving from one country to another—adjusting to different schools and systems. It wasn't that hard. When I was in San Francisco, Dan homeschooled me. He's a journalist, an author, and a freelance writer. Working from home allowed him to follow the curriculum that the Canadian schools followed.

The actual problem was Mom. She moved from one town to another when I was in San Francisco. I never knew where I'd be living once I headed back with her. For some reason, she always needs to switch her landscape and find new friends.

Mom and Dad are complete opposites. She's a nomad. Dad is pretty sedentary. When I look at my parents, I wonder if I'm going to end up like Mom, in love with love. Or like Dad, finding the love of my life and settling in.

"Is this why you're obsessed with soulmates? You want your children to have a more normal life?"

"Wow, that's deep. I've never thought about it. I have two loving parents." I stand up and take my empty dishes to the sink, then turn around and lean against the counter. "Three if you count Dan. I like to see people happy. If they're single, I want to know why they are alone. Are they chasing love, or avoiding it?"

Dan says I'm too mature for my age. He can't understand how I can be reckless and introspective all at the same time.

Eros studies my face and smiles.

"Are you chasing love or avoiding it?" he asks.

"Neither," I respond automatically. "I'm too young to entertain the idea. If some guy declares his undying love for me, I might run the other way."

"So, there's an age to finding your soulmate?"

"It's hard to know when you'll meet the person you're meant to be with. I'm open to the possibilities, but in the meantime, I like to have a taste of life."

"You believe there's one person for everyone, but you don't want to find yours just yet," he concludes.

"Yes," I say with conviction as I'm about to wash the dishes.

He sets his dishes in the sink and says, "You cooked, I'll do the dishes."

It seems fair, and I'm too tired to hold a plate. I might break the dishes, and what if they cost an arm and a leg?

Once he's done, Eros asks, "Are you ready to head to bed?"

I nod, still a little hesitant about how this night will turn out. When I spoke to his sister, she was super friendly. "Listen, I'm sure it's scary to have a guy approaching you and trying to help. My brother is safe. He's like a big puppy. Also, he worries a lot about people. You could stay at the airport, and he'll stay with you until your plane takes off. It'd be best if you two go to a dry, warm, and safe place to spend the next two days. I promise you'll be safe with him. If there's a problem, you can reach the doormen. They are there to help you in case of an emergency. You're safe."

She talked so fast it made me dizzy. I decided to stay at the airport, and if the guy wanted to do the same, I wouldn't be bothered. I was hesitant to accept the invitation and stalled for hours. Chatting with him made the time go by so fast, I never realized it was so late. I'm sure Dad and Dan are going to kill me for accepting this guy's invitation. I also think that if they found someone in my shoes, they'd help her.

We walk toward the bedrooms and pass what I guess is a room. There's a bed leaning against the wall, a bunch of boxes, and more artifacts like the ones in the living room. Is this guy, Gil, avoiding home? He has probably been doing it for years, but why?

There's an archeological site right in this apartment. If we could dig a little, we can find what makes him live on his own, share someone else's family, and stay away from home. Is this even home for him?

Eros opens the door to a room. "You're staying here tonight."

The waft of laundry detergent, cedarwood, and musk remind me of him.

"This is your room," I state. I turn to look at him. "I can take the couch."

"There are plenty of beds in this apartment," he assures me. His grin is starting to become my favorite thing. I wonder what it'd be like to kiss the dimple on his right cheek. "There are only two rooms with a lock and a bathroom. Gil's and mine."

"Where will you sleep?"

"As I said, there are other guest rooms. There's a cable where you can charge your phone right by my nightstand," he instructs. "See you in the morning, Liv."

"Thank you."

"Don't thank me," he says. "Just pay it forward."

Chapter Four

Olivia

IT FEELS like I just set my head on the pillow when my phone rings.

"Hello?" I yawn.

"Finally." Dad sighs with relief. "We've been calling you all night, and you haven't answered your phone."

I look at the screen, and indeed there are many missed calls from him and Dan. What's more surprising is that it's not two in the morning as I thought, but almost seven.

"This is the first time I heard it."

"Only you could sleep on a chair." He lets out a loud exhale. "We tried to buy you a ticket for today, but there aren't any planes going out until tomorrow. I guess you're lucky you found a seat for tomorrow's flight."

"Thank you for trying, but I'm going to be fine," I say as I breathe the scent of Eros.

I'm pretty sure I'm going to steal his pillow—a little souvenir from the weirdest couple of days of my life.

"Have you eaten anything?"

I stretch, push away the covers, and get out of the bed. I never lie to my parents. They aren't going to take this well either. Thinking fast on my feet, I ask Dad, "Can I speak to Dan?"

Dad makes a weird noise, and I hear him say, "She wants to talk to you."

"Good morning. Are you okay, sweetheart?" Dan asks with so much worry in his voice. I feel guilty for what I'm about to say.

I push the door open and head to the living room.

"Yes, I'm all right, but last night I did something Dad might not approve of," I confess and twist the truth. "This family offered to take me home."

So, it's a half-truth. Eros offered to take me home. I spoke to his sister. That makes them a family, right?

"That's very nice of them, but it's also dangerous, Olivia." His voice is firm. He's not upset, but he's disappointed.

I'd rather have Mom or Dad yell at me than disappointing Dan.

"Can I speak to them?"

"To whom?"

"The family," he explains.

"Well, they're sleeping. It'd be rude to wake anyone up. Why don't I ask them to call you when they wake up?" I offer.

"Please do so. We need you to be careful. I'll call around to try to get you a hotel room for the night."

"Dad's going to be upset, isn't he?"

"Look at this from his perspective, sweetheart. You took charge of your life, and so far, things have been bumpy. He's frustrated because there's nothing he can do to save you from everything that's been happening. It's out of his control. For a guy with OCD who loves his daughter very much, it is hard. I know you have to learn, live, and make mistakes to grow up, but as a parent, it is hard to be just an observer."

I'm not sure if I should apologize for wanting to make my own mistakes or if he's assuring me that this is part of some growing pains Dad and I have to go through. My parents have to let go while I need to learn how to do stuff on my own.

"Yesterday was long and difficult," I mumble. "It was hard to say yes to this offer, but it felt like the only answer to my prayers. I understand why you would disapprove, but I didn't make the decision lightly. It took me five hours to accept."

"They waited for you to accept?"

"Yes."

He sighs. "Make sure they call me so I can thank them, okay."

"I will," I agree before hanging up. "Love you, Dan."

"Love you too, sweetheart. Be safe, please."

I hang up and sigh with relief.

"Did you just lie to your parents?" The baritone voice makes me jump.

Eros is only a few steps away from me. He wears a T-shirt and a pair of basketball shorts.

"I tweaked the truth."

He snorts. "Obviously. My imaginary family and I invited you to stay is pretty believable. Tweaking is a lesser transgression than telling them a big fat lie."

"Like you've never lied to your parents." I roll my eyes.

"You'd have to meet them to understand why I don't lie to them," he answers. I'm intrigued about his statement.

"Are you lying to me about never—"

"No. I'm dead serious. Octavio and Edna Brassard are no ordinary parents," he states. "So, your parents are waiting for someone to call them to say, yes, your child is safe with us?"

I nod.

He shakes his head. "You're on your own, Pinocchio. I don't lie."

"You can't be serious."

"I don't need to lie. Therefore, I don't have the experience you require to convince your parents that you're staying at my family's place," he confesses with a boyish smile that melts my heart.

I toss my hands up in the air and plop onto the couch. "What am I supposed to do?"

"Let's have some breakfast and we'll figure something out. I'm great at avoiding confrontation." He takes my hand. Heat rushes to my face. Our eyes lock for a second, the weight of his gaze making me shiver. I feel a little flash of panic and I divert my gaze, almost running toward the kitchen.

"You okay?"

I nod, sucking on my bottom lip.

He smirks. "We have something in common?"

Does he want to kiss himself too?

"What is it?" I ask, opening the refrigerator. "You don't have milk."

"It's in the pantry," he says. "Do you want cereal or oatmeal? Those are our only choices. I usually grab some coffee and an instant oatmeal in the morning."

"Why is the milk in the pantry?"

He shows me a carton of rice milk.

"Are you allergic to milk?"

He shakes his head. "No. It's easier to store. I don't drink milk as often as many people. Cow's milk goes bad within days."

"Cereal is fine," I state. "Do you have tea?"

I take a couple of bowls, set them on the kitchen table, and search for spoons. In the meantime, he sets up the coffee maker and fills a mug with water before putting it in the microwave. The way we do things without even speaking feels strange. This guy is different from any other guy I have interacted with. It's probably because he's a year or two older than me. He's out of my league, but I sure want to know how he kisses.

"You never told me what we have in common," I say, breaking the silence.

"We're both terrible liars." He winks at me.

I laugh. Let's hope he doesn't know that I'm starting to develop a crush on him.

"So, what are you studying?" I try to sound casual and not like a teenager crazy in love with a hunk.

"Business," he answers. "How about you?"

I shrug.

"Still haven't decided on your major, huh," he states, pointing at me with his spoon. "I always knew what I wanted to do."

Taking a spoonful of cereal, I wonder if I should give him the long answer. He's used to being with more sophisticated girls who wouldn't be choking on words because they're flustered by his hotness.

"I feel like I have a little time before I do it. If not, I can always go for something general like Liberal Arts and study for a master's degree once I have decided what to do with my life."

"It's vague, but it sounds like a solid plan."

I smile proudly. If only my father could be as supportive as he is. Why is it that adults want us to decide our future during the most confusing years of our life?

He caresses my cheek with the back of his hand. Every cell in my body vibrates. I want him to have his hands all over my body. I press my legs together. What is happening to me?

"You're worried about your future, aren't you?"

"It's scary to think about it," I answer. There's a lot packed into that one sentence. I don't want to discuss it with him—or anyone.

"You have your entire life to figure it out," he says, and his voice is like a calming tonic. A hypnotic sound.

Before I can register what's happening, one of his hands is around my neck. His fingers thread through my hair. His other hand cups my face. His lips brush my cheek as they move to my mouth. I'm unsure on how to react. His lips move firmly and insistent against mine. It's the sexiest kiss I've ever had in my entire life. Tilting my head to one side, I part my lips, allowing his tongue to slip inside my mouth.

He deepens the kiss. I've never been so eager to kiss someone. The kiss is soft, even when I feel the most intense need in my core.

He pulls me closer to him. It's like we can't get enough of each other. Like he's parting my soul and trying to fill it with his essence. It's the most ardent kiss in the history of love. Or maybe I've never been kissed with such a passion that I feel like he's possessing me.

I should stop him. We don't know each other. But I can't pull away from him.

Chapter Five

Eros

THIS KISS.

It's wild, breathless, or maybe I'm getting used to sharing each other's breath. The best word to describe it is heavenly. The moment my lips touch hers, I'm lost in a blur of passion. The whimper she makes when I press her closer to me and deepen the kiss combusts me. The heat we create could stop the blizzard happening outside and even melt the multiple feet of snow that fell overnight.

It's taking me a lot of willpower to hold back.

I want to drag her to my room and devour her. The noises she lets out as our hands roam up and down our torsos are driving me crazy. I'm getting harder with every lick of her tongue. This isn't what I planned when I invited her to stay with me. I can't even remember why I did it. All I know is that I want her.

This beautiful girl got under my skin between the phone call with her father and preparing dinner last night. It was so fucking hard to fall asleep while I knew she was just a door away from me, sleeping. Walking into the living room and seeing her wearing nothing but a tiny pair of shorts and a thin tank top, it brought me to my knees.

"Liv," I mumble against her lips, breathing harshly, trying to regain my composure. "This isn't why I brought you to my place. I swear."

"I know," she whispers.

Her arms remain around my neck. We're so close together I feel her warm, soft breath caressing my face. She places a gentle kiss on my chin.

"This shouldn't happen," I continue, and the words sound empty. False.

What I want to say is, I need to be on top of you. Inside you. I need to touch you, your soul. I need... "We need to stop," I say, knowing it is the right thing.

Her hazel eyes stare at me. She gives me such an innocent look that makes my knees weak and my determination soft.

"Okay," she says, releasing me.

The voice comes across low and hurt.

"I'm not rejecting you," I vomit the words. There's no other way to describe what I'm doing. "It's just... you are trusting me, and I don't want to take advantage of you. Even when I want... no, I *need* to continue kissing you."

The smile she gives me makes my chest swell. "No one has ever kissed me like that," she confesses. Her voice is so low I can barely hear her.

It'd be easy to tell her that she hasn't been with someone who knows how to kiss. That'd be a lie. "I've never shared a kiss like that with anyone," I admit.

"In five years, what will you regret the most?" She licks her lips. "Stopping this moment or having an unforgettable memory?"

If our kiss was so perfect, I'm sure that sex with her is going to be a thousand times better. I can see myself regretting not living this moment as early as tomorrow morning—maybe as early as two hours from now.

"I'll regret that we stopped," I respond. "What about you?"

She gives me a shy, innocent smile. "Me too. I want this. I think it's perfect. Better than I had ever imagined. I want you."

The only words I can make out from what she said is, "I want you."

I feel like a child who's been given the golden ticket and is about to enter the candy factory. I'm about to taste her sweetness.

I draw her close to me and mumble in her ear, "Are you sure about this?" Then I kiss the soft spot on the back of her ear.

Olivia tilts her head and smiles. "One hundred percent," she assures me.

Lifting her chin, I place a slow, soft, sweet kiss against her parted, damp lips. I grab her hand, pulling her toward my bedroom. Heat races down my spine as I look at the unmade bed and imagine her body sprawled there. I glance at her and smile. I don't have to picture how she'll look. I'm about to watch the live show. This time, I'll be with her.

My cock is so fucking hard. I could just push her against the wall and fuck her.

I don't.

I want to savor her.

She wants perfect. I want to grant her wish.

This has to be slow. It's the first time we are together. I don't want to rush the moment. Taking her mouth, I kiss her slowly, gently pushing my tongue between her lips.

I thread my fingers through her silky hair and place the other hand on her ass, pulling her closer to me. I rub my hardness against her body. She groans with need.

We share an ache—a desire.

She tugs my T-shirt. I bend over so she can reach above my head. My lips miss her when we break contact. Instead of pulling her closer, I drag her tank top over her head. I release a ragged breath when I look at her beautiful breasts. They are perky. Her nipples are hard. I can't help myself and fill my hands with her tits.

I nestle my face down the side of her neck, running my lips along her throat, placing a kiss in between her cleavage.

My hands push down her tiny shorts. They're soaking wet, and surprise, she doesn't wear panties to bed. I'm loving that she mimics every move I make. I wonder if she'll go down on me after I'm done eating her pussy. I moan, just picturing her lustful eyes staring at me as I pump myself inside her mouth.

It's so bizarre how I have this need to possess her and at the same time to be gentle like she's fragile. One wrong move, and I'll break her. I want to reach beyond anything I've touched so far. I want to trace her soul with mine. Taste the fire within her, burn, and be consumed. There are so many feelings grasping my being. I'm confused, but I don't stop. I allow myself to enjoy every emotion that her touch produces. She can't seem to stop tracing every ridge of my muscles. The way she explores me makes my heart swell along with my cock.

I stop her and invite her to sit on the edge of my bed. Bending, I press my mouth against hers. My teeth fidget with her bottom lip. When I release her, I kneel in front of her, parting her legs. I don't waste any time. I press my tongue against her wet pussy. Making this good for her is getting harder as I want to devour her, but I do. I want to make this unforgettable for both of us. I lick and suck her tender flesh, pushing a finger inside her tight entrance.

"You feel so good, Liv," I groan.

"Eros," she moans my name, pressing her core against my hand. She rocks her hips against my finger. I push another finger. I increase the speed of my tongue laps and the thrusting of my fingers. Her body clenches around my fingers. Her cries fill my room. My name on her lips sounds like a prayer. Maybe it's a plea.

I stand up, walk to the nightstand, and grab a condom. Her bright eyes watch me as I roll it over my length.

Placing myself between her legs, I look into her eyes and ask, "Are you sure about this?"

She nods.

I press my cock against her heat. She's so fucking tight. I enter her slowly. Our gazes lock. I lower myself and capture her lips as I continue pushing myself inside her. Once her warmth wraps around my cock, the world stops. It's a strange feeling I can't describe. It's not enough, yet satiating, and so consuming.

It's the road to nirvana.

I place a kiss on her ear.

I feel the urgency to ask if she's okay. I do. "Are you okay?"

She's biting her lip. Her eyes shine. I'm not sure what it is about her that scares me and makes me want more of her. Gently, I roll my hips in and out. We find a rhythm. My hand slides between us, finding her sweet pearl.

Her screams, having her under me, her eyes shining bright like a thousand suns, take over my rationality. I begin to thrust faster. I release a guttural noise as her body clenches around me. She squeezes my cock. I explode. It's the big bang creating a new universe.

I could see us doing this for the rest of the day and into the night. This will be a memory I'll treasure forever.

Chapter Six

Olivia

THERE'S nothing like sleeping against the warmth of a muscular chest. I would exchange my teddy for him. Who knew the worst Monday of my life would turn into the best Tuesday of my life so far. Though I'm not saying that I'm in love with the guy.

I'm sore after having sex with him three times. Touching... who knew I would enjoy his touch so much. My heart beats almost as fast as it did yesterday just thinking of everything that we did.

God, I can't believe I gave my V-card to a total stranger.

What's gotten into me this week?

Dan is right. I can be reckless. At least I'll be one of the few who'll say my first time was perfect. I remember Holly telling me that her first time had been awkward and painful. Mine... well, I have nothing to compare it with, but I liked it a lot.

"Are you awake?" he mumbles against my ear.

"Yes," I whisper.

"I hate to say this, but we need to get ready if we want to catch our flights."

"Already?"

He dusts kisses on my neck. "I'm afraid it is time to leave our snow globe."

I turn around to look at him.

"These couple of days were truly unexpected," I confess. "Why do good things come to an end?"

He kisses my nose. "We'll never know. If you didn't live so far away, I might say let's try to see each other once in a while. Where do you plan to go to grad school?"

"Let me choose a college first," I say with a chuckle. "You sound like Dad. I might have a few early admission responses when I get to San Francisco, but I'm not ready to decide."

"Wait, you haven't chosen a college yet?" he asks, jumping out of bed. "I thought you said you were a senior. I kept wondering how you could be a senior without declaring a major."

"A senior in high school," I add.

"Please tell me you're at least eighteen." His voice is a mix of anger and fear.

"I am. I'll be nineteen early next year if you want to be technical."

He runs a hand through his hair. "Fuck. I mean... Jesus, I almost committed a crime."

"You're only a couple of years older than me," I argue.

"I'll be twenty-four next year, Olivia." He rubs the back of his neck. "This shouldn't have happened."

"So, what? I'm supposed to apologize because we didn't exchange birth records?" I say indignantly and leave the bed, heading toward the bathroom. "You won't take this away from me."

He is crazy if he thinks I'm going to apologize for what happened. My heart breaks a little. Not because I'm in love with him. Let's get real. This wasn't about love. It was about a boy and a girl who met and are attracted to each other. This felt right to me. I know there's someone out there for me, but I'm sure I won't find him at this age. And it's not Eros Zephier, or whatever his middle name is.

Eros might regret this day, but for me, it'll be a fond memory. I'll just erase the last few minutes.

I enter the shower, and he's right behind me.

"So, when you said 'died a virgin,' you weren't exaggerating like the rest of the stuff you said in the airport, were you?"

"Go away," I order. I'm glad I'm washing my hair and my eyes are closed. He can't see my red face and the anger that's brewing through my veins.

"I'm sorry. I overreacted." His voice is soft.

Rinsing my hair and removing the excess water on my face with my hands, I finally look at him.

"You're sorry, but you regret it."

He closes his eyes and presses his forehead against the tile wall. "I should know better. I should've been more careful with you."

"It was my choice too," I argue. "I'm not a kid. It's like I have to convince everyone that I'm an adult."

When he opens his eyes, he looks at me like I'm a kid. "Being an adult isn't what it's cracked up to be. It's more than choosing where to live, having sex, or eating ice cream for breakfast. All of those are choices. Choices you need to make thinking about the consequences. That's the bottom line. When you're a kid, you learn there are consequences, but you get a pass. Once you're on your own, you have to confront them. You live with them for the rest of your life."

"Another fancy way to call me a child."

He kisses my cheek. "No, just advice from a stranger that will remember you fondly."

"If I was older?"

"What's the question, Olivia?"

"If I was twenty-three or twenty-four"—I lick my lips—"would this be different?"

He shrugs. "I guess we'll never know."

Something is missing in this conversation. I feel like the story is incomplete. There's no closure. Or is this the kind of situation where there's no need for an ending? It was just a moment, and it's over? I have so many questions that I'm sure will never be answered by him. Maybe it's time and maturity. I'll find them in a few years.

It's not like I was hoping that this would go somewhere. He's the one who said, "I wish you were closer. Where are you going to be next?" Well, not with those words, but I feel like that's where the conversation was heading. To a place where two people about the same age were making the grownup decision to place a semicolon at the end of an unforgettable time they shared together.

He wouldn't do it with me. Me. I'm just a kid to him.

"You didn't need a fancy way to say goodbye," I state bitterly as I scrub my body with anger.

"Who knows?"

"Are we exchanging numbers?" I ask, rinsing my body.

"No."

"Then it's goodbye. Period!"

"Maybe I'll see you one day on the street. We'll have a cup of coffee. You'll tell me about your amazing life, how you found your soulmate, and leave again. You'll be like this big wave that crashes against the shore once or twice in a lifetime."

I turn off the water. He hands me a towel. He's still all nice and gentlemanly, even when he's telling me we'll never see each other again.

As I dry my body, I ask, "How about you? What will you tell me?"

"That I'm on top of the financial world. I probably have a wife, a couple of kids. Maybe I'm single. You believe that the future is already written. I think every decision changes the path we walk. I hope that whatever I tell you is good news."

Heading back into the room, I find my clothes, get dressed, and walk again toward him. I push myself on my tiptoes and kiss his cheek. "Thank you."

"For what?"

"Even if I never see you again, I'll never forget you."

Chapter Seven

Olivia

I REGRET NOT GOING BACK to my hotel room to change.

It's blazing hot. Dad and Dan weren't kidding when they said New York summers suck. I thought it was a way to keep me in California.

The asphalt is melting. My shoes are about to catch fire.

What was I thinking when I said, "I'll drop the bags and head to my meeting. I look ready for an interview."?

There's a vast difference between summer in San Francisco and summer in New York. It's like night and day—like Antarctica and hell.

The last time I was in New York City, there was a blizzard. I can't believe it's been more than three years since that happened. As I cross the street toward the coffee place where I agreed to meet Dad, I wonder if Eros still lives here.

While the taxi was driving on Park Avenue, I spotted the building where he lived. I still remember the morning when we headed silently to the airport. There was this awkward goodbye. I wish we had hugged. In retrospect, he was right. We should've exchanged more than family anecdotes and philosophical views before jumping into bed.

What can I say? I was young and inexperienced. I still don't regret sharing my first time with him. If it hadn't been Eros, it could've been some other guy who didn't know how to kiss or be kind and gentle. I'm one of the few who can say my first time was perfect.

"Olivia?" The deep, sexy voice makes my toes curl.

When I look up, a pair of espresso-colored eyes stare at me.

"Eros." My lips curl up in a smile. "What a surprise."

Studying him, I notice he's changed. He wears a pinstripe suit, a blue tie, and dress shoes. He's as tall as I remember. His sculpted features look more... male.

"What a surprise," he says, bending and hugging me. "I was just thinking about you earlier today."

"The psycho girl who got in your pants," I joke and wink at him.

He shakes his head. "I'm sorry about my overreaction."

"How are you?" I ask. "Rich, married, and with children?"

He scrubs his face with a hand, checks his watch, and glances at the coffee place. "Do you have time for coffee?"

"If you buy me an iced tea, I might spend a few minutes with you," I joke, then I point at his suit. "How can you wear that when it's scorching hot out here?"

"You get used to it," he says, holding the door open so I can go into the shop.

We both order a smoothie and take a seat at the farthest table. "So, what have you been up to?"

"I finished my master's degree. It wasn't hard to land a job. Gil has connections. I've been busy."

As he talks about what he's been doing for the past few years, I feel like we're falling back to that day when we met at the airport. This is like a conversation with a dear old friend who I saw last night. Time hasn't passed, and yet, a lot has happened to both of us.

His sisters are moving to Colorado where his parents live. His youngest sister is now in high school.

"How about the wife?" I point at his ring finger.

He wiggles his finger and says, "Still single, but I started dating a coworker."

"Nothing serious, but it might be the love of your life?" I arch an eyebrow.

"The obsession for the soulmate kind of love continues," he jokes. "How about you? Why are you in New York?"

"Other than stalking you?"

"Well, that's obvious." He winks at me.

"I'm looking at schools. After college, I want to start my master's degree in business."

He arches an eyebrow. "Business?"

"Dad hopes I'll take charge of his company at some point."

"What are you planning?"

"I've been doing some traveling." I don't tell him that his childhood stories inspired me to travel around the world, nor that it was easy to convince Dad and Dan to come along. "I have a vague idea of creating sustainable farms in places like central and north South

America, where the weather is warm almost all year around. Maybe create jobs and make sure the people get paid what's fair and not just pennies for their hard work."

He's staring at me attentively.

I wave my fingers. "I know, it's too vague. Just think of it as an idea that might sprout into a big conglomerate created to help the world."

His smirk appears. The dimple in his right cheek shows. My heart skips a little. His hand lifts, and he brushes a strand of my hair away from my face. The electricity his touch produces makes me jolt. It also proves that the chemistry between us wasn't some cabin fever hallucination. I felt it then, and I feel it now.

Well, it's one-sided, but still, the physical reaction toward him was—is—real.

"Where are you thinking of applying?"

"I might apply to Columbia University," I declare. "One of my Dad's friends gave me a tour and explained the program to me—after the interview."

He looks at me, then at his watch. "Where are you staying?"

"We have a suite at The Plaza. Dad and Dan are staying here for the weekend. I'm flying out tomorrow morning. I'm visiting Mom for a couple of weeks."

He stands up and looks at me. "Any chance I can see you tonight?"

I shrug. "Maybe."

"I'll drop by after work. What's your room number?"

"Ask the front desk to connect you to Otto Sierra's room when you arrive."

He bends and kisses my cheek. I close my eyes for a couple of beats and move away. What is it about him that makes me want to kiss him, hug him, rip off his clothes, and...?

Okay, let's hope he doesn't show tonight.

Chapter Eight

Olivia

AFTER SEEING EROS, I spend the day wondering if I should buy a new outfit, pretend that I don't feel well to avoid seeing him, or just have a drink with him in the lobby and then say goodbye for good.

Unknowingly, Dad chooses for me. He buys tickets to watch a Broadway show. I'm not a fan of musicals, but I go with him and Dan. I'm trying to keep him happy. He's not thrilled that after visiting Mom, I'm going to check out the University of Toronto.

If it were up to him, I'd go to Stanford or UCLA.

Staying in the suite waiting for Eros to visit would've been a thousand times better than two hours sitting cramped in a chair. Then again, what if he didn't even show? He has a girlfriend. Why does he even want to see me? It's Friday. He must be on a date and forgot about me. Okay, I can see I'm slightly bitter. He might not have a wife and children, but he has something to show. I don't have anything that says, "Look, I'm older."

When we enter the hotel, I spot Eros sitting on a leather couch. There's a tumbler filled with amber liquid on the table in front of him. His attention is on his phone. I'm unsure if I should go to him or ignore him. The concierge approaches us and says, "Ms. Sierra, the gentleman over there is waiting for you."

Dad cocks an eyebrow and stares at me. A second later, Eros is right in front of us. He's wearing a pair of jeans and a T-shirt that molds like a second skin against his torso.

"Eros Brassard. It is a pleasure to meet you, sir." He extends a hand to Dad, who shakes it. "Otto Sierra, and this is my husband, Dan."

Dan and Eros shake hands. "Nice to meet you, sir."

"Hi," I greet him.

"Would you like to take a walk around the city?"

"It's a little late, don't you think?" Dad says in a snippy tone.

"Otto." Dan shakes his head.

I kiss his cheek, then Dad's, and say, "I'll be back soon."

"Olivia," Dad grunts.

I wave and pull Eros with me.

"Sorry," I apologize, unsure if it's because of my father's scowl or for not being here when he arrived. "Were you waiting for long?"

"No. I had a few things to do at the office. The concierge told me you'd be arriving soon, so I chose to wait."

There's a red light, and while we are waiting for it to change, I glance at him and dare to ask, "No date night today with the girlfriend?"

"Things with Tiffany are just starting. We both work a lot, so it's convenient to grab something to eat when we have some free time or go for a drink on a Saturday night after finishing a long day at work," he pauses, "but it's nothing serious."

"You work on Saturday?"

He nods. "And Sunday. If I want to make it big, I have to work my ass off. Some weeks I work almost eighty hours."

The light changes, and as we start to walk, he grabs my hand. "It's kind of like paying my dues. Everyone has to do it."

"Obviously, I don't understand," I claim. "But that's a lot of time working on... I mean, who are you helping while you do it? I'm not judging."

I stop because maybe he's like Dad. My grandma was a single mother who had to work two or three jobs to pay the rent and bring food to the table. Dad worked hard since he was able to have a newspaper route. Though, in the past few years, he's changed the vision of his company. He went from being just a construction company to planning and building developments that are sustainable. He uses recycled material. They have solar panels, windmills, and so much more. I recall Eros's parents didn't have much money. Maybe he's a lot like Dad in that sense. They want to build a future where their families won't lack what they did.

"At some point, you might want to figure out a way to slow down before you turn forty and realize that you've been spending all your life working and not enjoying it."

He grins. "It's not all work. There's the occasional weekend when I go to Colorado to visit my family, hike a fourteener, and skydive."

"Where are we going?" I ask.

He shrugs. "Do we need a destination? I really don't have

anything in mind. I just wanted to catch up with you. Fifteen minutes wasn't enough."

"It wasn't."

"We could have a drink. There's a bar close by that's quiet." He arches his eyebrow. "You can drink, right?"

I burst into laughter. "I'm twenty-two."

"You're still a kid."

"And you're close to reaching senior citizen status." I shrug. "It's the circle of life."

"I'm not that old."

"I'm not that young," I argue. "I kind of understand why you freaked out, but also, you have to understand my side. After something so intense, you rejected me."

We go down a set of stairs. He opens a door, and there's a small bar with jazz music playing. The tables are small, and the people are older than I anticipated. I want to remark on the senior citizen joke, but I'm afraid I'll be offending some of the customers. They aren't that old, but they are a lot older than me.

We grab a table. He focuses his attention on me and asks, "What do you want to drink?"

"Tequila, chilled, and a glass of water."

He comes back with a beer and two glasses. When he sits down, he says, "It wasn't my intention to reject you. I was angry at myself, never at you. It was my responsibility to ask, 'Hey, how old are you?'"

"You didn't take advantage of me," I assure him. "Except for that outburst, it was perfect. I'm one of the few women who can say my first time was great."

His eyes open wide, his mouth too. "You're kidding me, right?"

I shake my head. "No."

"Isn't that something you cherish and save for... fuck, I feel like an asshole."

I reach out for his hand. "Please, don't feel bad. I was aware of what was happening. Having sex was something I never romanticized. Maybe it's because my friends kept complaining about it. How bad it was, how much it hurt. I thought, this guy cares, he kisses like no one else. Perhaps it won't be awful."

"Was it good?"

I try not to laugh, but I do. "That's my current problem. It was too good, and now I'm having trouble finding a guy. They don't even know how to kiss."

"You can thank my sister."

"Why?"

"She once complained about how bad her first and second times were. She said if guys were less into getting immediate gratification and more into making a woman feel wanted, they'd enjoy sex a lot more."

"You have those kinds of conversations with your sister?"

"I beg her to stop, but Persy likes to yap nonsense all the time." He moves his hand as if it's a puppet. "She complains about our parents, but like them, she has zero inhibitions or filters."

"That's something I wish I had, siblings."

"I have three sisters. You can take one or two," he jokes.

We talk some more about his sisters. He tells me that his parents separated last spring. Since they are teachers and have summers off, his dad took off to help Gil on an excavation.

"It's weird to be twenty-seven and hear that your parents might divorce."

"I don't remember much of my parents' marriage," I confess. "It'd be devastating if Dad and Dan suddenly say they are separating or divorcing."

"Because they're soulmates?"

I nod. "Maybe your parents are growing apart, and they haven't spent enough time to fall in love with who they are becoming."

He snaps his fingers. "This is why I didn't think about your age. You sound like an old soul."

I grin. "That's what Dan says all the time. I can be mature, but then, I can be reckless too."

My phone rings. "Hey, Dad."

"Just a reminder that your plane leaves at six in the morning. That means arriving at the airport at least at four. It's midnight."

"It can't be midnight." I frown.

Eros shows me his watch and shrugs. "Tell him we're on our way back."

"Thank you for the heads-up, Dad."

As we make our way back to the hotel, I explain why Dad is freaking out.

"It'd be best if you stay awake until you have to go to the airport," he suggests. "I do that all the time."

"Are you still living at Gil's?" I ask.

He shakes his head. "Nah. I could, but once I got a job, it felt wrong. It was like freeloading off of my parents. I moved into a small apartment in Brooklyn."

When we arrive at the hotel, I want to ask him to come upstairs with me. We could talk until I have to leave, just like he suggested.

"This is it," I mumble.

"Thank you for tonight. I forgot how nice it is to spend the evening chatting with you."

His eyes look at me intensely. He bends over, cups my chin, and gives me a soft, gentle kiss on the lips.

"So, this is it?"

He nods. "For now. I have the feeling that I'll see you again someday."

"Maybe you'll have the wife and the kids."

"And you'll have your shit figured out and not just ideas."

I toss my arms around his neck and hug him. He hugs me back, and his mouth finds mine. This is something I don't understand. Our mouths are like magnets attracting each other. His lips are so addictive. I can't get enough of them. It's hard to resist them. Impossible.

If things were different, maybe this could become a lot more. I wouldn't have to be wondering if the next guy I flirt with is a good kisser or would care about me. This guy is so easy to be around. Should I move to New York?

Not for a guy. I need to let it go—let him go. He has someone, and his life is all figured out. I have a lot to do before I can even think about my future.

"Goodbye," I say, taking a step back.

He kisses my cheek one more time. "It's not goodbye. It's see you around."

Chapter Nine

Eros

MEMORIAL DAY WEEKEND is one of my least favorite weekends of the year. Once my parents switched jobs and became teachers, they proclaimed this to be our family's official vacation. It sounds like fun, except it's more like a camping trip where we're not allowed to bring any electronics. It's just the six of us and nature.

"You should talk them into switching the location to somewhere more vacation-like and less primitive," I complain to my sisters.

Persy grins. "Next year you should join our parentcation," she offers.

My sisters go on vacation to some swanky resort a week before we have to spend time together in this nonsense that's called *The Vacation from Hell.*

"Hmm, let me think." I cup my chin and look up at the ceiling. "One week with the parents and my annoying sisters. Or two weeks with my annoying sisters. Such a difficult choice."

Nyx pushes me with her hip. "You're missing the fun. By the way, can we discuss Callie's tuition?"

"When do we have to pay?" I grunt.

Unlike us, Callie didn't get any scholarship money or grants to help her pay for college. She is a smart kid, but she doesn't like to work hard for her grades. Since we don't want her to end up with a pile of student debt, we decided to pitch in and pay for her college expenses. When I agreed to do this, I had a great job and a salary that allowed me to help my parents and sisters.

A month ago, I quit, packed my things, and moved to Colorado to be closer to my family. I'm jobless, and I only have so much money in my bank account.

"Not until August, but I want us to talk her into getting a job," Nyx states, and I sigh with relief. "I'm okay with paying her tuition and some of her expenses, but just some of them."

"I second it." I raise my hand.

Persy shakes her head. As she's about to say something, the airline announcer calls for some flight. We all go quiet, hoping that our plane has finally arrived and we'll be taking off soon. It hasn't.

"We could've driven to Wyoming," I complain. "Or we should've gone to Canada."

"Stop complaining," Nyx says, annoyed. "You think I'm okay spending all this time with the five of you? I heard our parents having sex. I won't be able to sleep ever again."

Persy and I laugh.

"Who thought going to North Cascades in Washington State was a good idea? I mean, we have National Parks—"

"Eros?"

I stop mid-sentence and turn to my left. A couple of feet away from me is Olivia. It's been a few years since the last time I saw her.

"Hey," I greet her.

My sisters exchange a look. Persy and Nyx are like twins. They look a lot alike, and they share a brain. Just a slight gesture, and they already had an entire conversation.

"What are you doing here?" She looks around the airport.

"It's a long story."

She looks at her phone. "Well, my flight doesn't leave for a couple of hours. I have time if you have time."

Persy says, "Oh, he has time." Then she turns to look at Nyx. "Let's find the pretzels."

Nyx agrees, and they disappear through the crowd.

"Please excuse them. They were raised by wolves."

"Your sisters?"

"Yes, the twin monsters." I point at them as they disappear in the crowd. "Yeah, the slightly tall one is Nyx. Persy is the sample size."

Olivia frowns. "She's my size."

I shrug. "There's nothing I can do to fix it, can I?"

She gives me a suspicious glare. "Are you coming or going?"

"We're heading back to Colorado." I sigh. "As soon as the stupid plane appears. Is your flight delayed too?"

She frowns and then shakes her head. "Oh no, I just arrived at the airport. I'm visiting my parents."

"What are you doing in Seattle?"

"I live here."

"What?" I tilt my head toward the shops. "Let me get you something to drink while you catch me up with what you've been doing. The last time I saw you, you were looking for grad schools."

We grab a smoothie and find a table where we can sit and chat.

"Where are your parents?" We both say at the same time and laugh.

"I'm heading to San Francisco," she explains. "It's Dan's birthday. Dad is throwing a big party. How about you?"

"I just ended the worst week of the year."

She gives me a worried look. I explain to her about this nightmarish vacation that starts on Memorial Day weekend.

"Sounds like fun," she states.

"Not when you have to share a tight space with my family. My parents have zero inhibitions. I have to deal with not one but four women. They don't allow electronics."

She grins. "So, your parents are back together?"

"Indeed. Persy worked her magic. They reconciled a couple of months ago." I pause, sip from my smoothie, and say, "You two would get along well. She is a therapist—a marriage counselor or something like that. She also has a blog where she discusses love, sex, and relationships."

"Sounds like fun. Maybe someday we'll sit down to chat about love, sex, and she can explain what happens if I feed you after midnight."

"I forgot she told you that the first time that you two chatted." I almost choke with laughter. "So, tell me, how is it that you live in Seattle?"

"I work and live in Redmond. I graduated a semester early from college and a semester earlier from grad school. I thought speeding up my studies would help me find my future." She takes a deep breath, and when she lets it out, she says, "I wish I had partied more and spent a couple more years in school."

"So, everything is still an idea?"

She grins and shakes her head. "I like what I do. I work at a non-profit. It's a lot better than interning for Dad. And unlike Dad, they pay me."

"How's your father?"

"He's doing well. He's also hoping that I'll take over his construction company someday."

I arch an eyebrow. "That's what he does?"

"The company is more complex, but that's the gist of it. Now tell me about you. How's New York, the luxury life, the wife, and the kids?"

I laugh. "I quit a couple of months ago and moved to Colorado."

"Wife and kids?"

"If I don't have a job or some stability, I doubt I can have a family."

She tsks. "That's an excuse. You just haven't met *the* girl of your dreams. Your other half. When you meet her, you're not going to care if you live in a hut or some luxury apartment. All you'll want is to share your life with her."

"It's not that easy," I argue.

"Let me get this straight," Liv pauses, takes a sip of her smoothie, and continues, "You quit your job without a plan, moved to Colorado, and are starting from zero. However, you think falling in love is more complicated than that."

She laughs.

"It's easier to quit and move."

"Only for you."

"No, Misty also quit and moved to Colorado," I use that as a defense. Maybe she'll agree with me.

"Who is Misty?"

"A college friend," I explain casually.

She arches an eyebrow and crosses her arms. "You followed her?"

My phone rings. When I check, it is a text from Nyx. It's time to leave.

I grab my backpack and look at Olivia. If only we could have a few more hours.

"It was nice seeing you," she says as we both stand up from our seats.

"Same." I pull her into my arms and hug her.

As if it's the most natural thing, I kiss her. I don't know why I need that little taste of her. A way to stay connected? Who knows, maybe I'm insane, and the next time I see her, I should steer away from her. The last time we met, I stopped seeing the woman I had started dating. It felt wrong to be with someone when the only person I could think of was Liv.

"Goodbye," she whispers.

"Until next time." I give her one last kiss on the forehead before releasing her and leaving.

When I find my family, Callie is complaining about her seat.

"I don't understand why I have to be in the middle of Mom and Dad. One of you should be there."

"Because you get to sit in the first row," I explain to her. "We're going to be at the back of the plane."

Callie huffs, stomps her foot, and heads to where our parents stand.

"She's becoming a brat," Nyx complains.

"Were we that annoying when we were her age?" Persy asks.

"You're still annoying, Persy," I remark.

She sticks her tongue out. "Who was that?"

I arch an eyebrow. "What are you talking about?"

"The pretty girl who came to say hello to *Eros*," Nyx adds.

"Oh, that's... this girl I met at the airport a few years back."

"The one stranded with you during the blizzard?" Nyx asks, then elbows Persy. "*Airport girl.*"

"No wonder she wasn't falling at his feet trying to get his attention."

"What are you talking about?"

"Every woman you meet wants to get you in bed. This one was perky and happy, but I can see that's her personality. She wasn't touching you and rubbing herself against you while you two were talking."

"Were you spying on me?"

"Just for a couple of minutes," Persy confesses. "So, we assume the airport girl is just a friend."

"More like someone I know. We don't know that much about each other." I'm not sure if that's a lie. There's a lot that I've learned about Liv throughout the years.

Liv is a spark in the night... she's so much. She's someone I like and who I'd love to see again. There's a special bond between us, but I definitely won't tell these two. They are going to give me a hard time.

"She's pretty," Nyx says. "I could see you settling down with someone like her."

"Let me figure out what I'm going to do next before you start setting me up," I warn her.

"I can't believe you quit without a plan," she says, exasperated. "Not only that, but you dragged your friend Misty along with you."

Nyx is wrong. I didn't drag Misty. My sisters swear she has a crush on me. She doesn't. We've known each other for years. There's a difference between being close and being in love.

I met Misty Wilfred in college. Getting along with her is effortless. We became friends within days. She reminded me of Nyx and Persy. Unlike those two, she's beautiful, funny, and easy-going. I don't remember if I was attracted to her when we met.

"Wait, that's not true. She found a job in Denver. It wasn't because of me."

Persy gives me a glance that says, I can't believe you're so gullible. "Misty followed you. She's in love with you."

"She's not."

"Oh, please." Nyx rolls her eyes. "Stop and smell the diehard crush for you. I wouldn't move to another state for any guy. She moved for you. At least she was smart enough to get a job before following you—unlike you."

"He wasn't happy in New York. I think it was wise," Persy intervenes.

"It'd be fine if he knew what he's doing next. You bought a house, a car, and... what is next?"

"I have some investments and savings. It's not like I came back to live with my parents. Give me a couple of months. I'll figure this out."

Chapter Ten

Eros

SO, things didn't turn out the way I imagined. Fuck, I can't even say as planned. Maybe Nyx was right. I should've had a strategy before I quit, packed my belongings, and changed my life drastically.

It's been almost three years since I left my steady, well-paying job because I thought I could do a lot better. Instead of moving forward, I'm taking several steps backward.

I'm a fucking failure. Eating through my savings isn't a good strategy either. Now it's time to snap out of my pipe dream and go back to what I do best, working for others. The options are limited. Today, I'm interviewing with a big consulting company in San Francisco. Getting this job isn't optional. I'm a few months from having to sell my house and move in with my parents.

What a fucking joke. From trying to avoid my parents' fate, I'll end up being forty and living in their basement.

San Francisco is my last chance to do something with my life. Will it be hard to move away from my family? Probably. I know it sounds terrible. What can I say? I got used to having my two sisters visiting me with food, decorating my house, and just making decisions for me.

Can I do all that on my own? Sure, but that keeps them entertained.

As I make my way through the San Francisco airport toward the exit, a woman bumps against my chest.

"Sorry," she says. Her gaze is locked to her phone.

Before I scold her for not paying attention to where she's going, I ask, "Are you okay, ma'am?"

The woman looks up at me and laughs.

My heart drums inside my chest when I realize it's Olivia. "Hi, Liv." I smile at her.

Would it be weird to say that earlier today, I thought about her? It's logical, right? This is where her father lives, and it's been too long since the last time we saw each other.

"I had a feeling that you were around," she states.

I lift both eyebrows. "You did, huh?"

She shrugs. "Ignore my quirkiness. What are you doing here?"

I sigh. "It's a long story."

"It always is with you. Are you coming in to town or about to leave?"

"Just arrived," I state.

She checks her phone and then looks up at me. "Where are you going?"

"Le Méridien Hotel," I state.

"Hmm, the Financial District?"

I nod.

"Interesting." She bites her lower lip. "Let's go. My car is in the parking lot. I'll give you a ride."

She takes off without waiting for a response. Actually, she didn't ask for my input. When did she become bossy?

I follow right behind her.

"So, they make cars your size?" I ask when we approach a small two-door sedan.

"Careful, or I'll tie you to the roof," she argues.

I laugh and shake my head.

"So, why are you here?" she asks once we're inside the car, buckled up.

"I have a job interview, and you?"

"I work for Dad." She sighs.

"But you didn't want to work for him," I state, confused.

"You were setting up a business, and yet, here we are," she refutes.

Olivia isn't wrong about it, and this makes me feel worse in some ways. When I met her, I remember telling her that being an adult had consequences. I forgot to tell her that sometimes we can't even do what we love. Sadly, she realized that all on her own.

"We're a pair, huh?"

We leave the parking lot and she nods. "Certainly. It's not like I'm taking over or doing this permanently. I have a few ideas for a business, but I need someone to back me up financially. Dad won't help me until I show I have enough experience to run a business. In other words, I'm still a child and he doesn't trust me."

"Or he's trying to convince you that you could develop the love of working for him."

She twists her lips slightly and makes a weird noise. "Why didn't I think of that?"

"Reverse psychology."

"You use that with your kids?"

"No kids yet, but I use it with my sisters who think they use it with me."

"Twisted."

"Oh, you have no idea." I snort.

"So why are you getting a job?"

"The three businesses I tried to set from the ground up didn't work out. I invested in a venture that seemed solid, but it wasn't. I'm broke, unemployed, and about to sell a kidney."

"You sound defeated."

"It's been three years. I am beyond desperate," I explain, exhaling harshly. Closing my eyes, I wonder if I forced the big break or if I never had a chance. "It's time to grow up and go back to work."

"You're giving up too soon."

"Says the woman who swore she'd never work for her father," I counteract.

"Touché." She chuckles. "In all fairness, I do it because he might be right about not having experience. I rather like having him teach me all he knows. After all, the guy built an empire from the ground up without anyone's help. One day I'll be savvy enough to start my company."

"What kind of company?"

"Some sort of trading business where I import and export sustainable products around the world that are paid at a fair price. It enrages me that individuals and companies buy products from third world countries and pay only pennies for them when they're making a two hundred percent profit off of them."

It upsets me just as much. That would be a great business. I can see myself doing that for a lifetime. Helping people while I help myself too. "Like what countries?"

"Let's say Costa Rica."

"Have I ever told you that's one of my favorite places in the world?" I ask.

"You did. It's one of mine too." When she stops at a red light, she turns to look at me briefly. "It'd be the first place I'd go and try to set this up. There are a lot of areas where you can set up sustainable farms. We can sell items to local businesses: craft food, beverages, and other products. We can export them to other countries, including the United States. The possibilities are endless. You find a craftsman that creates beautiful jewelry and find a buyer that will pay fairly and not just a couple of dollars and then resell the item for hundreds."

"It's a great idea. We need to polish it, and you have to work on your pitch skills if you want to get an investor on board."

"Clearly, which is why I'm working for Dad."

"I know where to find people, land, and... it's really doable." Gil has connections all around the world. I could help her with that part.

"Is it?"

"Definitely. It'd require a lot of planning and a huge investment though." I scratch my chin.

"Hey, if you get the money and get it started, I'll buy half of the company when it's established and I have the money."

"Didn't you hear that I'm broke?"

"Find an investor," she says, as if it's simple. "It's a lot better than working for some soul-sucking financial institution and going back to the hamster wheel."

She stops in front of a hotel. "Here we are. Do you have plans for tonight?"

"Probably. It seems like you are just making decisions for me."

She chuckles. "I'll pick you up at seven."

"You are bossy."

She waves at me. "Good luck with your interview."

Chapter Eleven

Eros

I PROBABLY ACED THE INTERVIEW, but I didn't like the place. It's back to wearing suits, making money for already wealthy people, and spending ten to twelve hours a day in the office.

I have another round of interviews tomorrow, and there's a test. A fucking test. What am I, twelve? I almost flipped them the finger and said, "Keep your fucking job." I would do it, of course. It irritated me to no end that they need to make sure I can perform according to the company's standards. Didn't they see my credentials?

When I arrive at the hotel, there's a message on the phone.

"Hi, it's Liv. I... I have to cancel tonight. Dad's in the hospital. Maybe I'll see you in a couple of years." Her voice is nothing like the woman I spoke with a few hours ago. She sounds broken. I want to reach out to her and make sure she's doing fine.

I call the front desk to see if they can track the number, but they don't have anyone who can look into it at the moment. If I want, they can help me tomorrow. Tomorrow might be too late. I decide to do my own detective work.

I google hospitals in San Francisco and start calling them. San Francisco General is the one that transfers me to Otto Sierra's room.

"Yes?" a female voice answers.

I believe it's Olivia, and I dare to say, "Liv?"

"Uh-huh," she answers.

"Good, I'm on my way. What room is your Dad in?"

"Who is this?"

"Eros."

She gives me directions on how to get to the room. It's easier if I go through the second entrance, take the first elevator to the third floor and go to the left. Twenty minutes after I hang up with her, I'm on my way to the hospital. It's not too far from the hotel, and I decide to walk instead of calling a cab or an Uber. Her directions are pretty on point. When I arrive at her father's room, I spot her right away. Olivia is on the phone barking orders. Her dad sleeps on the bed. Sitting by his side is his husband, Dan.

I knock on the open door. Liv turns around and waves at me. "If you have any questions, call me. I'll send you an email later tonight."

"How is he doing?"

She takes a deep breath. "According to the doctor, he's going to be fine. He had a heart attack and is having triple bypass surgery tomorrow morning." She swallows hard. "It sounds scary, but the doctors assured us that he'll be fine."

I step in, kiss her cheek and then shake Dan's hand. "How are you doing, sir? Is there anything I can bring you?"

He shakes his head. "Why don't you take her out to dinner?"

"You need to eat too, Dan."

"We can bring him something on our way back," I offer.

"I like that idea," Dan agrees.

"But what if you need me?" she argues.

I grab her hand, squeezing it reassuringly. "We won't go too far."

"You heard the doctor. He's stable." Dan looks at his watch. "If you leave now, you might skip the scene where your Dad complains about the bland food and demands coffee and a burger."

Olivia grins. "He's not going to like the change of diet, is he?"

Dan squeezes Otto's hand. "He'll survive. It's not like we're going vegan. Now, go get something to eat."

She kisses Dan's cheek. "Call me if you need me."

We leave the room, head to the elevator, and as we wait for it, she asks, "How did you find me?"

"I called every hospital in the city, asking for Otto Sierra," I answer.

She arches an eyebrow and says, "Wow, if I didn't know you, I'd be a little concerned."

"Listen to me, I sound like a stalker," I joke as we enter the elevator. "We should exchange numbers, or the next time you might be serving me with a restraining order."

She offers a sad smile. The sadness and the grief dim her face. It pains me to see her hurt. "Actually, you sound like a good friend. Thank you for coming. I'm trying to be strong for Dad and Dan. It's hard." Tears run down her face. The elevator doors slide open. As we step outside, she says, "I'm scared. What if something goes wrong? I can't lose him. We—"

I put my arms around her, set a kiss on top of her head, and pull her tight as she allows herself to grieve. Anything I say might not be enough, but I do my best to reassure her that everything will be fine. I wish I could do more to take the sadness away from her. A meal and some words might not be enough, but they'll have to do.

If either one of my parents had a near death experience, I'd be devastated, but I'd try to be strong for my family. That's what they expect from me, to be the rock they can lean on when things are bad.

Eventually, we make our way to a pub that's a couple of blocks from the hospital. I have fish and chips. She orders a Reuben sandwich.

"How was your interview?"

I sigh and tell her all about it.

"You don't want this job," she concludes.

"There's no other alternative."

"I could give you a job if you're so desperate," she offers.

"What kind of job?"

She shrugs. "I'd have to talk to human resources and see what they have for someone like you. It feels like you took a step forward and now you're about to take two steps back."

"Believe me, I'm past that. I don't think I can afford to wait any longer."

Her phone buzzes. She smiles.

"It's Dan. Dad is awake. He wants to see me."

I call the bartender, asking to bring Dan's food, which Olivia ordered earlier.

"Thank you again for coming over," she says. "It's good to have a friend around."

"Don't tell me you've become a hermit-workaholic," I try to joke.

She sighs. "Holly, my best friend, lives in Boston. We talked earlier, but she can't just take off work to be with me for the next week while I have a silent existential crisis. My college friends are sprinkled around the country. I hang out with people, but I wouldn't say they are part of my circle."

I hold her hand as we walk back to the hospital. There's not much I could say that'll make her feel better. I understand her. A lot of my friends live on the East Coast. We sometimes talk, we text often, and we try to meet twice a year.

Other than Misty, who moved to Colorado when I did, I don't have any close friends. If I move to San Francisco, this will prove to my sisters that they're wrong. Misty moved to Denver because of the job, not because she's in love with me. I look at Liv. Actually, if I move here, I'll be close to her. For some reason, the dreadful feeling is gone. Here's that silver lining. My parents might call it the window that opens when all the doors are shut.

"Well, I'm here for you," I say reassuringly.

"That means a lot to me."

When we enter the room, her father is staring at the food tray in front of him. "Hey, Dad!" she greets him and kisses the top of his head. "How are you feeling?"

He frowns at me. "I heard you were with your New York friend."

"Sir, it's nice to see you again. I wish it was under different circumstances."

"You and me both." He sighs and stares at the bag that Olivia holds. "Did you bring me some edible food?"

"No." Olivia hands the bag to Dan. "You have to eat what's on the tray. Didn't you hear the doctor? Only boiled veggies and grilled chicken."

"I'll eat outside," Dan says, kisses Otto's forehead, and looks at Olivia. "Call if you need me. I'll be in the waiting room."

Olivia's phone rings. She bites her lip. "It's the office."

"Answer. I'll stay with your dad."

Otto and I stare at each other. Suddenly, he asks, "Why are you here?"

"Olivia mentioned she was at the hospital and I wanted to be here for her."

He nods. "So, you came all the way from New York because you heard I'm in the hospital?"

"No. I live in Colorado, but I had a job interview here in San Francisco," I explain. "We were going to go out tonight."

He narrows his gaze. "What do you do for a living?"

I snort. "Currently? Nothing."

"That's reassuring. You don't understand how well it feels to learn that your little girl's boyfriend is unemployed."

I laugh. "We're just friends. As I said, I came to San Francisco to interview with a financial firm."

Unamused, he asks, "What were you doing before that?"

Does he understand that I am not his daughter's boyfriend? What's with the twenty questions? Yet, for some reason, I feel obligated to answer. "I tried to start up a few businesses, but none of them took off."

"When you set up a business, you have to be passionate about it. You can't just say, I'll start a chocolate factory because it pays well. You have to know all about chocolate. Love chocolate. Your heart has to be in what you're doing or it won't do well."

Is it crazy that he makes sense? None of what I've done in the past three years has been exciting for me. I was just doing it for the profits.

"I wish someone had told me that before I burned through my savings."

"It was an expensive lesson, wasn't it?" I nod. "I'll give you a free tip. When I decided to start my construction company, I was broke. I tried to get a loan, but there wasn't any bank that would take a chance on me. Dan had just received an advanced payment for one of his books. He offered it to me. He trusted me and believed in me. He knew building was my passion, and I wanted to do more than just build a house. I wanted to develop neighborhoods, cities... the sky was the limit. Find your passion and then find someone who believes in you. It's that simple."

"What are you two talking about?" Olivia enters.

"What was that call about?" her father inquires.

"It's Lulu, your assistant. She postponed all your meetings for next week. I'll be taking over while you recover."

"Thank you for doing it. Why don't you head home?" he suggests.

"I want to stay for the night."

"Go home, Liv," Dan says, as he enters the room. "You can be here tomorrow morning. The surgery is scheduled at nine. They're taking him at eight to prep him. There's no point in being here."

"They are right. Why don't I take you home?"

She stares at her dad. Olivia's shoulders slump slightly. "Fine, but you guys promise to call me if you need me?"

As we're heading toward the exit, she says, "I don't want to be alone tonight."

"Why don't you come with me to pick up my things? I need my suit for tomorrow's interview," I suggest.

"You don't have to do that."

"I want to do it, Liv," I insist. "Unless you're the San Francisco cutie serial killer."

She snorts. "I can't believe you still remember that."

"It's not every day that you come across a woman who might be attacked by a yeti, accuses you of being *the hottie serial killer,* and cooks you a delicious grilled cheese sandwich. All in the same night."

"She sounds like fun."

"She's the best," I agree, guiding her hand to my mouth and placing a kiss on the back of it.

Chapter Twelve

Eros

LIV'S APARTMENT is like her. Small, cute, and welcoming.

"Everything you own is tiny," I joke.

She glares at me. "Are you telling me you drive a big truck, own a mansion, and your furniture is for people over six feet tall?"

I roll my eyes. "I own a small SUV—which is a hybrid. My house isn't that big, and I'm sure there's no such thing as furniture for tall people." I pick up a frame that's on a bookshelf. "I love this picture of the three of you."

She stands between Dan and Otto. "The ears are very mousy," I joke.

She nods. "That's the day they took me to Disneyland before I left for Canada to stay with Mom."

"It must've been hard."

Olivia shrugs. "I got used to it. We talked every night. One thing I wish we had back then was video calls." She studies me for a couple of seconds before she says, "Well, it's not much different from your childhood. I can't imagine what it'd be like to grow up jumping from one country to another. For you, it was perfectly normal."

"Adaptation," I answer. "We didn't know any different. I get it."

She walks me to a bedroom. "This is where you're staying." Then she points to the room at the end of the small hallway. "If you need anything, I'll be there."

"Do you have to be in bed before eight?" I joke. "I thought we were going to hang out at least until midnight."

"No, I'm just giving you a tour of the place. I'm hopping in the shower. It's been a long day." She wrinkles her nose. "I still smell like a plane."

"Planes don't smell."

"They do. It's a kerosene and dirty-bathroom scent," she says with conviction and heads to her room. "The next time you fly, pay attention."

"Maybe the planes I take don't smell," I dispute.

"Or your sense of smell is terrible," she suggests, giving me a face that says, I can't help you, buddy. "So, when are you heading back home?"

"Thursday afternoon," I answer, placing my things in the empty closet.

"Well, if you get the job and end up moving to San Fran, I can sublease you this room," she offers and claps excitedly. "We could be roomies."

"It's very kind of you to offer, roomie."

She comes out of her room holding some clothes and a towel. "It's the least I could do for you. Though, I still think that you should start your business."

"*Your* business, so you can buy it from me when you're ready?"

"I'd only buy half of it." She touches the handle of the door that's across from my room. "This is the bathroom. The clean towels are under the sink. I don't have cute toiletries like a hotel, but feel free to use mine."

"So, I can smell like flowers and sunshine?"

She bites her bottom lip, hiding a smile. "It's a lot better than airplane fuel."

"Somehow, I think you're telling me that I stink." I smell my arms and my armpits. "Thank you for making me feel self-conscious."

"In all seriousness, thank you for staying with me tonight. I couldn't handle being alone."

I step closer to her, lift her chin, and kiss her nose. "You don't need to thank me. I'm just glad I'm here for you."

"It's like you appear from nowhere to save the day."

"I'd like to differ. I'm just keeping you company. Something tells me that you're not the kind of woman who needs a knight." I give her a peck on the lips.

Her bright eyes stare at me for a couple of beats, then she enters the bathroom, shutting the door right away.

I DON'T OWN PAJAMAS. I sleep naked unless I'm at someone else's home. It never occurred to me that I'd end up staying at Liv's house during this trip. Sure, I thought about her when I realized I'd be traveling to San Francisco. That doesn't mean I planned on seeing her. Though, I'm glad we crossed paths. It's always fun to catch up with her. More importantly, I would hate to know that she had to be alone tonight.

The whole idea of not having anything to wear around the house but jeans and a couple of suits is uncomfortable. Thankfully, I find a pair of gym shorts shoved in a pocket. They don't smell bad—or at all. I guess this will have to do for the night.

After Olivia comes out of the bathroom, I head inside to shower. The bathroom reminds me a lot of my sisters' who leave their cosmetics on the counter. Persy is living with Nyx for a few months, and I've been avoiding visiting them. Unlike the fruity shit my sisters use to bathe, Olivia's smells fresh. Citrus, ginger, and ocean. I can live with that.

When I come out, Liv is setting a couple of mugs on the coffee table. "I wasn't sure if you'd want some hot cocoa, but I prepared one for you just in case."

"Does it have enough marshmallows?" I study the mugs.

"Sorry, I don't have any."

I stare at her with eyes wide open. "Blasphemy. How can you drink hot cocoa without marshmallows?"

She grins. "What can I say? Every time I buy a marshmallow bag, I finish them all in one sitting while binge-watching a show. When I have chocolates, I combine them."

The face she makes reminds me of her sex face. Damn, it's been so long, and I can still remember that day. I shake my head. This isn't the time to bring up old memories or jump in bed with her. She's in a vulnerable state.

Use your big head, Eros.

"Let's talk about this business idea you have, but you want me to start. I hope you know that doesn't make any sense," I say, redirecting the conversation to a safe subject.

She heads to her room for her laptop. I do the same.

"Can I connect to your wi-fi?"

"The wi-fi password is YetisArereal#1. The *y* and the first *a* are uppercase."

I burst into laughter, remembering the first time we met and how I had to explain to her they're part of the Himalayan folklore. "You're kidding me?"

"Nope. You can argue as much as you want, Mr. Wikipedia, but that's my truth." She challenges me with her gaze. "They. Are. Real. My password confirms it."

"I don't care if you have a pet unicorn. Just give me *the real* password so I can connect," I dismiss her challenge.

"I already told you. You can be skeptical and remain in the dark."

When I type it into my computer, it approves it. I glare at her. "But they aren't real."

"For a well-traveled man, your mind is too limited." She laughs. "Plus, my passwords can't be hacked by boring people like you."

"Let me guess. Your computer's password is: Iminlovewithaleprechaun69?"

I'm enjoying her laughter. We're not making sense, but at least she's relaxing. After we compose ourselves, she tells me more about her idea. We argue the pros and cons. I google a few things for preliminary research. I plan on getting in touch with Gil to see if he can help me with some of his connections.

We spend most of the night brainstorming names for the company, the mission statement, and the places where we could set it up.

It's around two in the morning when I realize she's fallen asleep. I shut down our computers. Carefully, I pick her up from the couch, set her on top of her bed, and cover her with the folded blanket that's on top of the comforter.

"Sweet dreams," I whisper, kissing the top of her head.

As I pick up my laptop, I notice the screen of her phone is illuminated. I grab it and read part of Dan's text to her. "*Sleep well. Try to be here around seven. Your—*"

That's all I can read. I wonder if her Dad is all right or if that's the time they'll be taking him to prep him for surgery. But what if it's something else? Dan would've called if it was an emergency. My first interview isn't until nine. I'll wake up early, drive with her to the hospital, and wait until I know her dad is okay.

What is it about her that pulls me to her? It's like destiny keeps bringing us together for one reason or another. I look at my computer and wonder if this trip wasn't about the job but the business idea. I'll talk to her about it tomorrow. I'm invested, but this is her brainchild. I can't just take it away.

Chapter Thirteen

Eros

THE TEXT WASN'T AN EMERGENCY. Otto wants to see her before they prep him for the surgery. When we arrive at the hospital, Otto and Dan are hugging. The scene is tender and heartbreaking too. The sadness weighing on Dan is palpable.

"Do you mind if I have a word with Liv?" I'm pretty sure he's talking to Dan, but he definitely doesn't want me there.

Instead of waiting for Liv, I head to the coffee shop across the street. I order two lattes and a tea. The three times Liv and I have been at a coffee shop, she asked for tea or smoothies. I buy a few pastries and head back with the drinks and food.

"Are they still talking?" I ask Dan.

He nods a couple of times.

"Here, I brought a latte for you." I extend the cup holder.

He grabs a coffee and stares at the tray. "Liv prefers tea."

I smile, feeling good about my choice. "No worries, that's what I brought her."

"Thank you for looking after Liv last night," he mumbles. "I wish I could split myself in two. She's afraid of losing her dad."

"You're afraid of losing both," I guess.

He looks at me and sighs. "There's no reason for her to stick around if he's gone."

"Otto isn't going to die, but if he does, she wouldn't leave you. You're her dad too. She adores you as much as she loves her other two parents," I assure him. "This isn't something she's told me. It is what I've observed."

He stares at the floor and takes a sip of his coffee. "We never talked about it. I fell in love with her the moment I met her. I never regretted leaving Otto because I wanted her to have a happy family. When he came back to me, I didn't know what my role was. I never asked, afraid he'd say you're nothing to her. I just tried to be a part of her life. I love her as if she's mine. She's so loving and happy. Also, she's a part of him."

"Concentrate on Otto's recovery. Then you three might want to talk about your family," I suggest.

He's about to speak when Liv comes out. Her eyes are red and swollen. She's so broken.

"Dan, he wants to talk to you." She sniffs.

He hugs her. "It's going to be okay, sweetheart. I promise. Nothing is going to happen to him." After kissing the top of her head, he enters the room and closes the door behind him.

"Everything is going to be fine," I assure her.

"Dad gave me instructions in case he doesn't make it." She sniffs.

I set the cups and pastries on a chair and take her into my arms. I press her against my body, trying to create a cocoon to protect her from this moment.

She's gasping for air. "Why do I feel like I can't breathe?"

"Take in some air and count to six before you exhale," I order, cupping her face. I connect our gazes. "You are okay. Otto is going to be fine. In about six hours, he'll come out of surgery good as new. Do you believe me?"

She closes her eyes and nods once. I press a gentle kiss on each eyelid, then her nose, and I brush my lips against hers. I can't help myself. I slant my mouth on hers and kiss her. I'm not sure what I want to accomplish with this kiss. I want to take away her pain, give her my oxygen, or make her forget for a moment that life is unfair. The sound of the door handle moving makes me stop immediately.

Olivia's attention goes to her shoes. Her breathing is shallow, but the tears are gone. I release her.

"Liv," Dan's voice is a low whisper. "He's going to be okay. He promised me he'd be okay."

"I don't know what we'll do if we lose him." She sniffs. "I can't lose either one of my parents. You three are all I have."

Dan hugs her, closes his eyes, and kisses the top of her head. "We'll be around for years. Otto is going to be fine."

I squeeze his shoulder lightly. "Of course, he will, and then you'll be fighting with him because he's going to demand his bacon, and you'll be giving him cantaloupe with ricotta cheese instead."

There's no way I can leave them by themselves while Otto is in surgery. I excuse myself and go outside the hospital to make a couple of calls. It's easy to switch my flight.

When I try to reschedule the interview, I'm told that it's impossible. They have stronger candidates for the position whose salary matches what they are offering. In other words, they weren't planning on paying me what I asked for. I should take another look at Liv's idea. I could try to approach Gil and see if he could lend me the money.

Around lunchtime, I run to the pub for sandwiches and drinks for the three of us. Liv barely touches her food. Dan doesn't even acknowledge it. According to the doctor, the surgery could last up to six hours, and it's been only three.

"At what time is your interview?" Liv asks.

"I canceled it," I respond.

She gasps. "Why? I can lend you my car."

"I don't want to leave you."

"Have I told you that you're like some kind of guardian angel?"

"Maybe I'm a guardian yeti." I wink at her.

"But the job..." she mumbles. "I'm so sorry."

I lift her chin and give her a peck. "Hey, it's fine. It wasn't for me. Maybe we'll figure out a way to start the other business."

"Dad needs me to run his company." She gives me a sad smile. Leaning her head against my chest, she whispers, "Promise you'll make it happen."

"Promise that one day you'll come and work for me, and we have a deal."

OTTO COMES out of surgery around two o'clock. The doctor gives Dan and Liv a timeline. He should be sitting up by tomorrow afternoon. He'll stay in the Cardiac Care Unit for a couple of days before being taken to his room. They are going to discharge him five days after he leaves the CCU. Liv and Dan begin to make plans. She's taking over the company while he'll be in charge of Otto's recovery.

Around five, they're allowed to see Otto. We stay at the hospital until eight when Dan makes us go away.

"Thank you for today," Liv says when we enter her apartment. "I don't know what I would've done without you."

I caress her forehead with my thumb. "I don't like to see you frown."

She smiles. "You're leaving tomorrow."

I shake my head. "No. I'm staying for a couple of weeks."

"Why?"

"Because I need you to be okay before I leave," I explain, crushing my mouth against hers.

This time, I don't hold back like I did in the hospital. I have this need to absorb her. She kisses me back just as hungrily. The craving is mutual, but is she in the right state of mind?

"Liv." I rest my forehead on top of hers. "We have to stop."

I'm aching. I want her so much, but this time I don't want to fuck things up like I did when we met.

"Why?"

"I don't want to take advantage of you," I say.

"I'm not eighteen anymore," she claims. "Please, don't make me feel like a fool."

"I want to do the right thing," I insist.

"Then erase everything that happened today," she pleads. "Let this be the only memory I have of this day. You're good at it."

I take her mouth. Our tongues twist together like old friends who haven't seen each other. Two lovers who had to be apart for so long but are finally together. It feels like it's been a lifetime, maybe billions of years since the last time we were like this. Today, I want to make up for the time we wasted. Why is it that I have this big pull toward her?

Chapter Fourteen

Olivia

THE DAYS that follow Dad's heart attack aren't as exhausting as the doctor told us. I guess it's because Eros stays with us. It's been nice to have another person to lean on during these dark times. More so when we spend some time together either planning his business or having sex. Who knew both could be so gratifying, fun, and relaxing?

Dan, Eros, and I take turns being with Dad while he's in the CCU. By Saturday evening, they discharge him from there and transfer him to a regular room. If we're lucky, he'll go home by Wednesday.

"Otto is settled in, resting. Why don't you guys take the night off?" Dan suggests.

"It's my turn to stay with him," Eros says with a voice between a warning, a protest, and an order. He's cute when he tries to be in charge—and hot. "You need to go home and rest, Dan."

"We have an extra bed here," Dan points at the cot that's next to Dad's bed. "I want to stay with him. I appreciate you guys, but I need to be with him."

Eros smiles. "I understand. My parents would be requesting the same if the other one was in a hospital bed."

"I'll see you tomorrow after lunch. Maybe you can stay with him for a couple of hours while I go home to get another change of clothes," he says.

"Are you sure, Dan?"

He bobs his head. "Positive, sweetheart." He looks at Eros. "Why don't you guys go out and have some fun. This boy has been here for several days, and you've only shown him the inside of a hospital."

"It's a fine hospital, sir," Eros jokes.

We say goodbye to Dad and Dan before heading to the car.

"Where do you want to go?" Eros asks, opening the passenger door for me.

"Home?"

"That's what I was thinking." He gives me a mischievous look, hugs my waist, and presses me close to him. "I can eat you first, and then we can order some takeout."

He kisses me like he's never kissed me before. I'm getting used to having him with me all the time. In a way, I wish he had gotten the job. We could've been a lot more than just roommates. I avoid thinking about his departure and our future. Like Dad told me before his surgery, live every moment and don't obsess about the future.

So, this is me, just giving in to the kiss, the night, and the next days with Eros. But how I wished it could be an eternity with him, instead.

MORNINGS WITH EROS seem to be just as good as our nights. Dan was right. It's weird that Eros has spent his time in San Francisco between the hospital and my house.

"We should do something touristy today," I suggest.

"If you give me a choice, the only one I want to explore is you." He touches my inner thigh all the way to my center. He nibbles my ear. "You're ready."

"Stop, I'm serious." I jiggle and protest. "I feel awful that you spent your time in San Francisco with me."

"Why? Am I such bad company?"

"Not what I meant." I kiss him. God, I can't get enough of him. I touch his bare chest. "If Dad wasn't sick, what would you be doing?"

He cocks an eyebrow. "I would probably be home—alone. Who knows? If I were home... Let's see, it's Sunday. It depends on who needs me. Some weekends, Mom goes to the nursery with my sisters to buy new plants. So, I guess I'd be gardening with her. I'm the one who ends up moving things around and fixing the landscape. If Dad wants to fix things around the house, I need to be there to help. He had a hip replacement six months ago. He can't carry stuff. You're right, I'd be doing something more entertaining than being with boring ol' you."

He pulls me on top of him. I grind my hips against his shaft and lean over to kiss him. My mind is trying to forget about the outside world. It's been four days of Eros and Olivia inside a bubble. There's no work, no obligations, and no deadlines. Other than visiting Dad, it's just us.

But what if there's someone else? Someone he hasn't talked about who is waiting for him in Colorado.

I lift up my hips, reaching in between my legs and pushing his length inside me. This isn't the time to think about Friday when he leaves and we go back to being nothing but a distant memory.

"What's going on, Liv?"

I shake my head. He chuckles.

"What are you laughing at?" I try to sound angry. The pleasure oozing through my pores makes it impossible to be mad at him. If anything, I'm grateful for his kindness. I am a little enamored because not only is he hot and a sex god, he's also easy to get along with.

It'd be too easy to fall in love with him. How would it be to share more than just a few nights with him?

"You're thinking," he states.

"What? I'm not allowed to think when we're together," I argue. He's wrong if he thinks a lot is going on inside my head. It's hard to think about anything while we're together. Well, except thinking about us not being together—which is what I'm doing.

Are you? Because you were just pondering how easy it'd be to fall in love with him. Not only that, but what would it take to make things happen between the two of you.

"Not when we're like this," he claims, flipping me over and slipping back inside me.

"So, I know we said you're clean, and I am too... I'm on the pill." Nothing says this is us better than our awkward, oops, we didn't talk about this before it happened conversations. Like when he woke me up at three in the morning and we had sex.

It's so, so good. Also so, so *unprotected.*

He arches an eyebrow. "I'm not with anyone, Liv. I wouldn't be here with you if I was with another woman. It's been a long time since I've done anything, let alone date anyone. Also, you're the first person I've gone bare with."

"It's just that this feels so intimate," I mumble. "I've never..."

I chew on my lip because there haven't been many guys after him. One. So really, this is a lot for me to take while he—I don't even want to know how much experience he has.

"Me neither," he assures me. "This is special. Ours."

I close my eyes, briefly sucking in that word. *Ours.* My eyes open wide immediately because... "What's going to happen after? Fuck, I feel like some needy woman who's asking for a lot. I just want to know if anything will happen. You live there. I live here."

He nuzzles my neck. "You're not needy. We'll figure something out."

We begin to rock our bodies against each other slowly. Every time we're together, it is different. It can be rough, rushed, urgent. Against the wall. Bent over the table. In the shower. This time we're not rushing the moment. But every time, he thrusts hard, claiming me. My pussy clenches around his cock. The world stops when we're like this. The only sounds are of the two of us moaning, kissing, and touching the most intimate parts of ourselves.

ON THURSDAY, Dad is discharged from the hospital. The doctor gives us instructions for his care. He should be able to be up and about within twelve weeks. However, Dan made him promise that he won't go back to the office for a year. They're going to spend the next few months together enjoying each other and adopting a healthier lifestyle.

I'm officially in charge of his company. That thing I refused to do. Ironic, isn't it?

"This view is fucking amazing." Eros stares at the Golden Gate Bridge. "I wouldn't mind working from here."

"You're hired."

"Though I'm thankful for your offer, I'm sure you'll regret it by Monday."

"What are you going to do next?"

He turns to look at me and smiles. "I found what I'm passionate about. I just need to make it work."

"You will," I assure him, but in some ways, I feel like this is the part of the story where we have to go our separate ways. The last day we share something special. I'm afraid that we'll never see each other again. Or maybe... "Do you think the next time we see each other we'll be able to say, I'm finally on top of the world?"

"Well, I have your number, so we can text often. I don't see the need to wait until the next time serendipity pushes us back into one place, do you?" he questions.

I shake my head.

"Maybe I could visit you often, and you could—"

"No," I stop him.

"What?"

"You're about to say let's try to have a long-distance relationship, aren't you?"

He grins. "I don't even know what I wanted to offer," he confesses. "We're both in a weird place in our lives."

"Plus, I don't believe in long-distance relationships."

"Have you ever tried it?"

I nod. "At the end of my freshman year in high school, I dated this cute sophomore. Mom had plans to travel with her friends. She sent me to California earlier than usual. He was dating someone else within three weeks." I shrug.

"We're not kids."

"No, but we're both busy. How often are we going to call each other, text, or even see each other?" I argue.

"But we can be friends, right?"

"Always, Eros."

He takes my hand, pulling me out of my chair and into his arms, and kisses me hard. As if this might be the last kiss we share for the rest of our lives.

Chapter Fifteen

Eros

"WHY DO I feel like I haven't seen you in weeks?" Persy asks when she enters my house.

I look up from my computer. "Would it be because *we haven't seen each other in a couple of weeks?*"

"Someone is touchy today," she complains.

"No, just busy," I answer.

There are days like today that I want to ask her to hand me the keys to my house.

"What are you doing?"

"Are you bored?" I ask, grabbing my coffee mug.

"No, just doing some research," she answers, taking a seat. "You've been busy. What are you working on?"

"A proposal." I grunt.

Can she leave?

Eros: *Do you still want one of my sisters?*

Liv: *You can't just give them away like souvenirs. Why are you asking?*

Eros: *Persy is at my house. She's a classic case of pain in the ass.*

It's been a day since I came back from San Francisco, but it feels like weeks. I miss Liv in a way I never imagined would be possible. I have conflicting thoughts about her and our time together. I wish I had stayed. All the emotions she provokes terrify me, yet, pull me to her.

Who knows what would've happened if she had agreed to try to have a long distance relationship. I don't even know why I suggested it.

Who am I kidding?

I like her—a lot.

I want her.

I almost need her like I need oxygen.

Liv isn't just any person. She is a cyclone of emotions. Colorful and happy as a wildflower. She's a flame that brands my soul every time we touch. Her light is so intense, I want to walk toward her and run away at the same time.

My heart wants to surrender to her. My head keeps reminding me that I'm not ready to be with anyone. Let alone *her*.

The ambiguity couldn't be clearer—or more confusing.

That's Olivia Evelyn to me.

The most beautiful chaos who might be best to admire from afar.

Which is why I'm sticking to talking about safe subjects from now on. Liv and I have been texting since I made my way through the airport security checkpoint. We've been discussing her new position and my new business. I want to make sure I follow her vision. It's important to me that she has some input.

"What kind of proposal?"

I move my gaze from the monitor toward her. "A business proposal."

She narrows her gaze. "Another one? I thought you were giving up."

"Do you want me to give up?" I lift my mug.

"No. I'm the one who said do some research and find something you'd really like to do."

"Well, that's what I'm doing." I drink my coffee.

She bobs her head a couple of times. "Do you use sex toys or masturbate with your hands?"

I spit the coffee all over my computer and my monitor. "Fuck, Persephone. Can you at least give me a warning that you're about to be inappropriate?"

She gestures her hands as if she's about to choke me. "Didn't I just tell you I'm doing research?"

"That can mean so many things with you," I say as I clean my computer and the table. "What is this nonsense for?"

"Next week's podcast. I got an email from a listener asking if I had any recommendations for male toys."

I blink a couple of times. "You're not going to leave until I answer, are you?"

She grins.

Eros: *Hey, she needs me to answer a few questions. This might take longer than I thought.*

Liv: *Is this for her podcast?*

Eros: *NO!*

Liv: I'm so looking forward to hearing what her brother did this time.

Eros: How do you know?

Liv: I've been listening to her podcast. I'm on season 2, week 29.

Eros: I regret telling you about it.

Liv: I'm loving it. Your family is a hoot. I feel like I know everyone. Is it true that you caught your parents having sex in the back of your car?

Eros: Ironic, isn't it?

Liv: Hilarious. I'm sorry about her breakup with Ian. They looked like a cute couple.

Eros: Liv, did you stalk my sister?

Liv: I was bored. While I listened to her podcast, I read her blog and looked at her pictures on social media. You seem to have a great relationship with her.

Eros: If you don't count the times I want to wring her neck.

Liv: I'll be around when you're ready.

I close my laptop and look at Persy. "Honestly, it's the first time I'm aware that there are sex toys for men."

She twists her lips and types on her phone. "How many times have you played with sex toys?"

"By myself, never. I might've done it once with a woman I dated in New York," I answer.

She taps the table. "How often do you have one-night stands?"

"Not as often as you think," I answer vaguely.

My sisters want me to settle down. I don't have time for that. Sometimes I just need to tell them that I like to play the field. Let's be honest, I don't have the time or the money to be playing anything. Dating is expensive and time consuming. I am not in the market to waste either one for something frivolous. That's something I allowed myself to do in my mid-twenties, and even then, I didn't do it as much as I bragged.

"So, you're not too adventurous in bed," she concludes.

The memories of everything I did with Liv the past few days come to mind. Not using a condom was in a way more adventurous than having sex on the balcony. We explored things she's never done. Things neither one of us had tried before. I told her about the book I bought my parents—*Sixtysutra*, Kamasutra for seniors. We googled the regular poses. I wish I had had more time to try all of them.

"How can you measure how adventurous people are?" I challenge her. "Do sexologists test couples and individuals? I didn't know you had a kink, Persephone. No wonder you enjoy your job."

"You're an idiot." She huffs.

"I'm right. You can't measure it."

"Well, some might say that those who are into threesomes, orgies, or swinging are adventurous. While others consider using toys with partners or by themselves just as bold." She leans closer. "Which category are you in?"

"Neither."

"I need to place you in one of those," she insists.

"Why do I have the feeling that you're going to portray me on your show as something I'm not?"

"Because women love to know about my brother's love life—even if I have to make something up," she says, tapping her phone. "Let's talk about the last woman you were with. How long did you wait before having sex with her?"

"I refuse to answer."

"Why? It's not like she'd know." She arches an eyebrow. "She'd know that you told me, wouldn't she?"

"What have you been posting about me?"

She shrugs. "Nothing you haven't authorized before. It's like today. I ask questions. You respond to them. If I don't like it, I tell you what I'm going to say. Then, I discuss everything with my audience."

"And you want to tell your audience that I have my own toy collection?"

"Listen, I might get a few sponsors that will offer to pay us if you try their products. What do you think?"

"No."

"I'll give you the money they pay," she offers.

I rub my chin. "How much are we talking about here?"

"It depends. Sheila gets twenty percent of that, but I can give you the rest," she offers. "You'll just have to report how you used them."

Before I can answer, the main door opens, and it's Nyx. She points at me. "Where have you been?"

"The last time I checked, here," I respond vaguely.

"No, you weren't here all week. I've been calling you since last Friday, and you've been sending me to voicemail." She shows me the house keys. "I came to check on you, and your car was gone. All week."

"Stalker much?"

"Eros, where were you?" she insists.

"Out of town."

"And you didn't tell us?" Persy asks, surprised.

"Why did you leave?" Nyx crosses her arms.

"I didn't know I was grounded, Mom."

"You and Persy were ignoring my calls," she complains. "I ended up co-signing Callie's lease."

"Don't blame me," Persy defends herself. "I already told you, you shouldn't have done it."

"Aren't you living with her?" I ask Persy, confused. "How come she couldn't find you?"

"I was in LA with Sheila," she responds. "I did answer her phone call and told her not to sign that lease. She didn't listen."

Nyx sighs and closes her eyes for a couple of seconds. "Well, what was I supposed to do?"

Persy and I shrug.

"Exactly. Someone had to do it." She rolls her eyes and goes to the kitchen. After grabbing what I assume is a cup of coffee, she heads toward the stairs. "I'm going to use your printer."

"She's pissed."

"Mostly with our parents," Persy says. "They enable Callie, and then they expect us to fix her shit."

She gives me that curious look. "So, where were you?"

"I went to San Francisco."

"Why?"

"This is off the record, right?" I want to make sure that she won't be posting my crappy life. She nods. "I had a job interview."

"That's... far," she pauses. "Why not try to get one here in Denver?"

"I already tried. It's almost impossible. Either I have too much experience, or they can't pay my salary."

Her shoulders slump. "Are you moving?"

"I don't think so." I tell her about the business idea. The conversations I had with Otto. He's a wise man with a lot of experience. I omit some parts, including Liv. Persy doesn't need to know about my complicated friendship with Olivia.

"That's great advice," Persy says after I tell her what Otto said to me about doing what I love. "It's also true. I do what I love, and I'm soaring."

I arch an eyebrow. "So, you're telling me I should start a podcast and talk about sex?"

She slaps my arm playfully. "You never take anything seriously."

"Life is better when you laugh at your own misery."

"I had no idea you've been miserable since birth."

"Why do I put up with you, Joy?" I call her by one of her middle names.

"Because you love me," she concludes. "This business sounds like something you'd enjoy. What do you need to start it?"

I show her the spreadsheet with the budget. "I need seed money to launch it."

"How long will it take you to pay it back?"

"I don't know, a year or two. It all depends on the return." I show her the three possible scenarios.

Liv helped me a lot with the vision and the business plan. While I was in San Francisco, I made a few calls. Gil, my godfather, liked the idea. He said he'd loan me the money if he hadn't invested it all in producing a show. If I can wait a couple of years, he'd love to be a part of this venture. However, he promised to help me with his contacts. He agreed that I should start it in Costa Rica. He also has a few ideas for where I could expand the company once it's profitable.

I reached out to a couple of friends from grad school, hoping that they'd know a good investor.

They promised to be on the lookout.

Nyx returns with two piles of papers. One for Persy and the other one for me.

"I made a few notes. Tell Sheila that I need her to revise the other contract." Then she looks at me and taps the papers in front of me. "Sign these papers and initial where I put the little flags. I came to an agreement with the guys from Juicestart. You won't sue them if they return half of your investment."

I sigh. That money buys me more time to find an investor. "You're the best sister ever."

She huffs and heads upstairs again.

"I angered the beast," I joke.

"Stop mocking her. It's been a stressful week for her."

"What happened?"

"Callie. Her behavior toward Nyx is irritating."

"One of us has to make her understand that we aren't Callie's parents," I suggest. "And that one shouldn't be me."

She laughs. "Says the man/child of the family."

"Ouch."

"Jokes aside, if you ever need money, I'll loan it to you." She looks again at the spreadsheets. "It's doable."

I shake my head.

She squeezes my hand. "I believe in my big brother. Maybe it's time you believe in yourself too."

Chapter Sixteen

EROS: *What do you think about the new plan?*

Liv: *I'm just reading it. Some of us need a little more time to read through a document.*

Eros: *How's your Dad doing?*

Liv: *Better. He's not happy about his "new lifestyle." He hates fish and boiled chicken.*

Eros: *I wouldn't want to be your dad.*

Liv: *I'm thinking of becoming a vegetarian. Did you know that his condition could be hereditary?*

Eros: *Why not pescatarian?*

Liv: Hmm. Why didn't I think of that? I could do that and sneak a cheeseburger once a year.

Liv: Once a month.

Liv: If I make sure my pizza has the same ratio of carne asada and poblano pepper, would that be a balanced diet?

Eros: I still think that's a weird combo. Who puts salsa verde on a pizza? It's supposed to have marinara sauce.

Liv: Yet, you ate it all when I made it.

Eros: I was hungry.

Liv: You loved it. Next time you visit me, I'll make you more.

Eros: Have you ever thought about ordering pizza? It saves you time.

Liv: Where's the fun in that?

Eros: Do I have to fly to San Fran and teach you how to have fun?

Liv: Is that a promise?

Eros: I would do it if I wasn't in the middle of this project and you weren't trying to figure out how to run the company and keep your father away.

Liv: Dan worries me. He has to live with the man. If I were him, I'd be planning my escape.

Eros: What happened to that soulmate gibberish you presume exists?

Liv: I guess this is the test of true love.

Eros: How are you dealing?

Liv: I'm getting used to receiving a million calls from Dad. The man likes to micromanage. Juggling my job, his, and keeping him happy and away from work is more challenging than I thought.

Eros: Great practice for when you become your own boss.

Liv: Ha! I might be stuck with this company forever.

Eros: I thought you were going to work for me.

Liv: I said I'd buy half of it once I have money and it's success-ful. I'd be your boss. (kidding)

Liv: Any leads about the silent investors?

Eros: No, but my little sister offered to loan me the money.

Liv: The lawyer or the sex guru?

Eros: I should tell her you called her a sex guru. Persy is the one who offered it.

Liv: She's a wise woman. While I'm single, I can use her exper-tise to keep myself entertained. I even bought some of her toys. Unlike you, some of us do want to have fun. :ROFL emoji:

Eros: I can't believe she mentioned that I didn't know there were male sex toys.

Liv: You should see all the comments on her blog post. Women and men are willing to teach you how to use them.

Eros: Are you done laughing at me?

Liv: Fine, I'll stop. Just don't be surprised about your birthday present.

Eros: That's next week.

Liv: There are seven days next week, which one.

Eros: May first.

Liv: You're a May Day baby. :ROFL emoji:

Eros: Stop laughing at me. Yes, I am. My sisters like to bug me about it too. Have I mentioned you'd get along with the twin monsters?

Liv: How about the little one?

Eros: She's complicated. There's an age gap between us that, for some reason, isn't closing as she gets older. But maybe you'd get along with her too.

Liv: We'll see. As for the money, if I were you, I'd take the loan from Persy.

Eros: In the back of my mind I keep asking myself, but what if it fails?

Liv: *Toss those negative thoughts away. I believe in you.*

Eros: *I guess these past few years did a number on my self-confidence.*

Liv: *Time to straighten up, dust off those knees, and keep going. Listen, I hate to go but Dad's calling me.*

Eros: *Good luck!*

FROM: **E. Brassard**

To: **O. Sierra**

Subject: **Land**

Gil owns some land in Costa Rica. He's leasing it to the company. I'm booking a flight to Costa Rica for the second week of June. Would you like to join me?

I'm attaching the blueprints and all the information that Gil sent me about the place.

E.

FROM: **O. Sierra**

To: **E. Brassard**

Subject: **RE: Land**

I love the location. I hate that I have to decline your invitation. If I leave my post, Dad will try to take back his company. (Apparently, I've snatched it from beneath his almost dying corpse and I'm destroying his legacy with all my nonsense.) Dan likes to call this stage three of his recovery. You might ask, what is he recovering from? Workaholism. He's in the stage of anger.

Send me pictures and maybe a souvenir. (By that, I don't mean your sisters.)

Liv x

LIV: Happy Birthday, old man. Ready for your AARP card?

Eros: What is that?

Liv: The discount card for people fifty and older.

Eros: Oh, that. I'm not THAT old, OLIVIA EVELYN.

Liv: Old enough to need a hearing aid and shout like an old man.

Eros: Is this how you show your love and appreciation for your friends and family?

Liv: Only to my elders. Will you ever tell me how life was during the last century, Grandpa?

Eros: That's it, I'm changing my number.

Liv: How's your day going, Grandpa?

Eros: I just came back from my morning run. You're actually the first one to congratulate me. Why are you up so early?

Liv: We're having issues in Boston.

Eros: You have a project in Boston?

Liv: Yes, and a branch.

Eros: How big is this company?

Liv: Google it. We have branches in many cities, including one in Colorado.

Eros: That can be an excuse to visit me.

Liv: Surprisingly, that branch does well. They don't need me there.

Eros: So, any hopes of talking you into coming to Costa Rica with me? It'd be a great birthday present.

Liv: Sorry, not happening. Happy Birthday though.

Eros: *Thank you for the text.*

Liv: *I'll try to connect tonight unless you're busy.*

Eros: *We're having dinner at my parents'. You're invited if you can make it by six.*

Liv: *Maybe another year. I gotta go. Have a wonderful day.*

Chapter Seventeen

EROS: This year's family trip was entertaining.

    Liv: Well, hello to you too. It's been a long time since I heard from you.

    Eros: I told you I'd be gone for a week.

    Liv: You did?

    Eros: I sent you an email last week about it. You emailed me back with your suggestions and said, text me when you're home.

    Liv: Oops, I only opened the attachment. I didn't read the rest. No wonder you didn't text me that night, or the next day, or... you get the idea.

Eros: I don't know how to reply to that.

Liv: Just tell me about this trip. Is this the one you take every Memorial Day weekend?

Eros: Yes, that one.

Liv: What happened?

Eros: Callie brought her boyfriend. Some preppy guy who is out of touch with reality. His name starts with a J and we began to joke about it. I can't remember if it was Jarred, Joshua, Jonathan, or what. He caught my parents having sex.

Liv: So those jokes about catching your parents naked and doing it aren't just some propaganda for Persy's show?

Eros: Unfortunately, no. They are all real.

Liv: I'd die if I caught my parents having sex.

Eros: It is traumatizing.

Liv: So, what happened with the boyfriend?

Eros: They broke up. Apparently, we're too much to handle.

Liv: How long had they've been together?

Eros: I'm not sure. Maybe three months?

Liv: And she brought him on a family trip? There must be some dating rule about not introducing the parents to your significant other until you are comfortable enough to show the crazy. You can't include them in family events until you've been together for a year. A camping trip? I wouldn't know, but definitely more than a year.

Eros: I couldn't agree more. I doubt I'd bring any girl to them, like ever.

Liv: Not even the wife?

Eros: Maybe when our children are eighteen and can fend for themselves.

Liv: Have you ever introduced anyone to them?

Eros: I've never had a long-term relationship, so nope.

Liv: Interesting. Why not?

Eros: I don't have time. There's a lot involved in having a steady and committed relationship.

Liv: So, you just sleep around?

Eros: Can I plead the fifth?

Liv: This isn't a trial, but if you don't want to answer, I'll give you a pass. Now, tell me more about the trip.

Eros: Well, after the guy left, everything snowballed.

Liv: Are you giving me details?

Eros: I teased Callie for the rest of the week. Nyx was trying to micromanage everyone. She loves Persy, but she'd like to have her privacy back. As you well know, I borrowed Persy's savings. She can't afford a down payment or the deposit for a new place, at least not until she gets her quarterly royalties. Nyx isn't happy that I'm yet to start another business that might fail. She also wants Callie to get a real job or apply for a master's degree.

Liv: Isn't that something your parents should be telling you?

Eros: Nyx thinks it's her responsibility to do that. She is also like one of those mothers who says, "I believe in you, but are you sure you're doing the right thing? I have a feeling that this won't be successful—like all your ideas. Do something safe."

Liv: Does she know she's not your mother?

Eros: She believes that if she doesn't take charge of us, we'll be drowning. She's afraid of failure. I adore her, but she needs a chill pill. No. She needs to fail to understand that not everything has to be perfect.

Liv: That's deep.

Eros: How are you?

Liv: I'm well. Dad and Dan are traveling during the summer. I'm officially in charge of the company. I'm the interim president.

Eros: Interim president? That only applies to politics.

Liv: Listen, if the guy wants to call himself the president of his company, it's his choice.

Eros: I should be the emperor of my company.

Liv: Ha!

Eros: Fine, you can be the empress. I'll be the god.

Liv: Why don't you stick to CEO?

Eros: Too conventional, but if that's what you want, I'll use it.

Liv: So where is Persy going to live?

Eros: Her agent got her a nice place. I have to help her move this weekend. In the meantime, she gets to live with the 'rents.

Liv: Why didn't you offer her a room?

Eros: I'm a slob. Her words, not mine.

Liv: So, I dodged the roomie bullet, huh?

Eros: I'm not a slob. They haven't lived with me for years. During our family trips, I leave my stuff all over the place. It's a great way to bother them without even trying.

Liv: I have the feeling that you're different with your family than you are with the outside world. You behave like a big child when you're with them.

Eros: It's fun. So, about Costa Rica...

Liv: I already told you, I can't go.

Eros: You can't blame a guy for trying. It's been a couple of months since the last time I saw you.

Liv: Why don't you come out to San Fran?

Eros: As soon as this business takes off, you'll be the first person I'll visit.

Liv: Who'll be the second one?

Eros: Probably you.

Liv: I might think that you miss me.

Eros: Am I not allowed to miss you?

Liv: It'd be best to keep this platonic. Two friends who help each other with work and text fun stuff.

Eros: So, I can't ask what you're wearing.

Liv: Just like I won't answer with something like, I'm not wearing any panties.

Eros: That means you're in pajamas. Are you wearing one of the T-shirts you stole from me?

Liv: I didn't steal them. You left them behind.

Eros: You promised to wash them, and I never saw them again.

Liv: Hey, I need to send a few emails to Dad before leaving the office. Can I text you when I get home?

Eros: Liv, it's ten. YOU SHOULD BE HOME.

Liv: It's nine in San Fran, but yes. I'll leave after I'm done.

Eros: Text me before you leave the building. Take care of yourself. x

---

LIV: Your sister is kidding, isn't she?

Eros: What sister and about what?

Liv: Persy... your parents were having sex in the kitchen?

Eros: Yep. You should've heard her yelling like she just saw the biggest spider in the world.

Liv: And what about what your dad said about the juicy...?

Eros: All true.

Liv: They are putting the Sixtysutra book to good use.

Eros: I don't think my sisters appreciate the present I gave them for Christmas.

Liv: Your sister is right. Who wouldn't want to be sixty and still be passionately in love?

Eros: If we're single by the time we're sixty, we can be each other's sex buddies.

Liv: Why am I single at sixty?

Liv: Are you calling me damaged goods?

Liv: Do you think I'm unlovable?

Eros: *Sheesh... I didn't mean it that way.*

Liv: *How did you mean it?*

Eros: *I was trying to be nice.*

Liv: *Because you think I'm going to end up single. A spinster. I won't even have nieces and nephews to pity me.*

Eros: *I'm sorry. I didn't mean to offend you.*

Liv: *You at least have your sisters who might give you a niece or two. I'll have to start collecting cats, and when I die, I'll have them buried with me like the Egyptians used to do with their pets.*

Eros: *You're laughing at me, aren't you?*

Liv: *You're so easy.*

Eros: *Just for that, I'll get someone else to be my fuck buddy when I'm an old man.*

Liv: *Nah, you'll find that wife and procreate a gazillion gods with her.*

Eros: *I think two children are plenty.*

Liv: *Why not three? Two boys and a girl.*

Eros: *Poor kids. That little girl is going to boss them around.*

Liv: *Speaking about sisters, where are you?*

Eros: *At home, and you?*

Liv: *On a Saturday?*

Eros: *I had a text date with you. Why are you asking?*

Liv: *I just saw that your sisters are at a bar, partying. I thought you were with them.*

Eros: *Nope. Persy was organizing some kind of newly single party for Callie. I thought that was going to be at Nyx's house.*

Liv: *I haven't partied much since I moved out of Seattle.*

Eros: *Did you party when you were in Seattle?*

Liv: *Some. I used to work for a non-profit. The owner's son is a former bandmate of the band Sinners of Seattle. They usually invited us to a bar when they played.*

Eros: *Look at you hanging with famous people.*

Liv: I doubt they knew who I was. Once I came to work for Dad, I stopped going out often.

Eros: You said there's a branch here in Colorado. Why don't you run the company from here and I'll teach you how to party.

Liv: Rafting in the morning and vegging at night?

Eros: You know it. I'll even let you make pizza for us.

Eros: Ugh, I need to go.

Liv: Are you okay?

Eros: My sisters need me to pick them up. They're wasted. I'll text you once they're safe.

Liv: K. Drive safe. x

Chapter Eighteen

FROM: E. Brassard
To: O. Sierra
Subject: New direction
Hi,

I'm sending you the revised business plan. I made a few modifications to comply with the investors. I'm returning Persy's money this week. After I get the funds, and if all goes well, this company should be profitable within two years. That's scenario B. Let me know if you want to make any changes.

I hope your trip to Boston was prolific and that you'll come to Colorado soon.

It's going to be weird to work with someone Persy is dating, but beggars can't be choosers.

E.

LIV: I'm confused by your last email. Do you need money?

Eros: *No. I said I'm paying back Persy's loan. I found a silent partner who'll invest in the company. Nyx helped me negotiate the contract (so I won't lose my house).*

Liv: *Still confused. What does Persy's boyfriend have to do with the project? More importantly, where did she find her boyfriend? I've been following her blog and social media for weeks. Other than the few losers she went out with, I haven't seen anyone worth the trouble.*

Eros: *Sometimes I learn more about my sister's life from you than from her.*

Liv: *What can I say? I'm fascinated by your family. You guys are... peculiar. So, about the boyfriend?*

Eros: *He and his brother have an investment company. I'm partnering with them.*

Liv: *So, the trip to Costa Rica is still a go, or do you have to postpone it again?*

Eros: *I'm postponing it until September. Nate wants to go with me.*

Liv: *And Nate is?*

Eros: *One of my silent partners.*

Liv: *Phew. For a moment, I thought that the past four months of work were going into the trash.*

Eros: *Do you want to join me?*

Liv: Even though I'd love to, I can't. Dad's staying away from the company until May of next year.

Eros: He's never coming back, and you're the next president of the company.

Liv: Nope. I already told him that once he's back, I'm taking some time off.

Eros: What are you planning on doing?

Liv: Who knows? I might move to Boston with Holly.

Eros: Why Boston and not Colorado?

Liv: It's just a joke. I need a plan before I take off.

Eros: You have a job with me when you're ready.

Liv: I'll think about it.

EROS: My sister is pregnant.

Liv: I'm not judging, but didn't she just start dating this guy a couple of weeks ago? That's anatomically impossible. Or is it biologically?

Eros: Not Persy. Nyx.

Liv: Congratulations, Uncle Eros!

Eros: Thank you.

Liv: How is she? Happy, I'm sure.

Eros: She says she's okay, but I'm not sure. She was fired, and her former boss threatened to disbar her. She took off with my silent partner.

Liv: All that happened to her in just one week?

Eros: Three days. It's bad.

Liv: She'll be fine.

Eros: It's Nyx. She doesn't just take off and leave things up in the air. I'm worried.

Liv: You said it before, she needs to make mistakes to learn that life isn't perfect. A baby is never a mistake, but getting fired might be the key to her happiness.

Eros: Nate is not her happiness. This guy is cool. He does have a crush on her, but I hope that he stays away from her for everybody's sake.

Liv: Why?

Eros: He's a playboy. How serious can he be about a single mom?

Liv: He might surprise you. Have you found Callie?

Eros: Nope. The last time she answered my call, she told me to go fuck myself. Who packs her shit, doesn't tell her family, and leaves to... who the fuck knows where she's at?

Liv: This big brother thing might drive you to drink or to the grave. Are you still worried about Persy and her new boyfriend?

Eros: No. I like him.

Liv: One out of three sisters doing well isn't bad.

Eros: Since you're a soulmate-love expert, can you answer my question?

Liv: I can't see if there's love in your future. Are you feeling like a spinster?

Eros: No. It's not about me.

Liv: Shoot.

Eros: So, there's this guy who's been friends with this girl for years. They are close. She has a serious boyfriend, and he just realized she might be the one who got away.

Liv: I don't see the question in there.

Eros: Persy and I have been discussing this subject. She says the guy isn't in love. That it's not possible. I insist that it can happen.

Liv: You want me to be the impartial judge?

Eros: The voice of reason.

Liv: Why the sudden interest in her?

Eros: It's hypothetical. I wouldn't know the answer.

Liv: I'd need to know more about this. There's a possibility that he finally fell for his best friend. But if the woman in question is in love with her boyfriend, he should stay away. He had his chance and blew it.

Eros: This is like an entire third option.

Liv: Sorry, but the reason why he suddenly notices her doesn't matter. If she's happy and he really cares about her, he should shut up and stay away. He had his chance.

Eros: You're telling me that even if this woman is the love of his life, he has to step aside?

Liv: If indeed she was such, he'd have noticed her a long time ago.

Eros: I feel like you're siding with Persy.

Liv: I think both of you have valid points.

Eros: Hey, Dad's asking me to help him fix his truck. Talk to you later.

Liv: Run from reality. You know I'm right.

Eros: You're not. Put a pin in that conversation. We'll get back to it.

LIV: Sorry I missed your call.

Eros: No worries, I just wanted to say hi. I'm at the airport.

Liv: This is so exciting. I wish I was with you.

Eros: You can still come with me.

Liv: The Boston branch is a mess. I fired the manager. Dad's going to have another heart attack when he finds out about it.

Eros: You should've done that a couple of months ago. (I told you so.) Do you need any help?

Liv: Just send me pictures and keep me updated. I want to live vicariously through you.

Eros: I still don't understand why you can't come to work for me.

Liv: Don't tell anyone, but I might like working for Dad. After all, I'm in charge. : wink emoji :

Eros: Don't work too much.

Liv: K

EROS: I'm back!

Liv: I was promised more pictures.

Eros: I'll upload all the pictures I took to the cloud. My phone doesn't work in the area. There's no signal or cell tower.

Liv: Well, that sucks. You're going to be out of touch more often than I expected.

Eros: How are you?

Liv: I'm doing well. I heard that Persy is making a few changes to her podcast. Is she okay?

Eros: She's making sure that people stay away from her personal life. Her boyfriend is a very private person.

Liv: In my opinion, she could just talk about her brother. It's fun when she makes fun of you.

Eros: Remind me never to introduce you to my sisters.

Liv: I might send her a Dear Abby letter.

Dear Persy, I have this friend whose sister always talks about her brother on her blog or podcast. Is there a way she can tell more embarrassing stories on the air?

Sincerely,

Eros's Friend.

Eros: Can I cancel our friendship?

Liv: You could, but then your life will be filled with sadness.

Who will you reach out to when you want to complain about your sisters?

Eros: *I'm going to stay in Costa Rica forever. That way, neither one of you can bug me.*

Liv: *I'll find you.*

Eros: *Empty promises. How's Boston?*

Liv: *Still a mess. I was there last week. On the plus side, I got to see Holly. I'm trying to convince her husband to work for me. He's an architect.*

Eros: *If there's anything I can do to help you, let me know.*

Liv: *Why don't you upload those pictures so we can talk about them. That'll keep my mind busy and away from work.*

EROS: Nyx is having a girl!

Liv: *That's so exciting!*

Eros: *Yes, it is. She's coming to Colorado with Nate. Persy's birthday is this weekend. She and Ford are moving to their new house.*

Liv: *Sounds like fun. I've always wanted to be at a big family reunion.*

Eros: *Why haven't you been to one?*

Liv: *Dad doesn't have siblings or cousins. Grandma died when I was nine. Dan's family lives on the East Coast. The years I was with them, we never went to visit them. Mom's family never organized one. I visited my grandmother twice a month and during the holidays when I was in Canada and she was alive.*

Eros: *When we were younger, we visited my grandparents every holiday. They always organized big parties. One day I'll bring you over so you can have the Brassard experience. A word of caution, we're not easy.*

Liv: I already figured that out. How's the company?

Eros: Going well. Gil is in Costa Rica, giving me a hand. It's the first time I've seen him excited about something that's not an archeological discovery.

Liv: So, I was watching this documentary about the ruins of Machu Picchu with Charles Gil. He looked familiar.

Eros: He's my godfather.

Liv: That's what I thought. So, his last name is Gil?

Eros: Yes. I've no idea why everyone calls him by his last name.

Liv: I hate to stop this chat, but I have a meeting.

Eros: It's a shame that you can't multitask.

Liv: I can but not when Dad is in the meeting. He knows when I'm a little distracted. Talk to you soon.

Eros: I'll text you later tonight.

Chapter Nineteen

EROS: *We're going to visit Callie.*

Liv: I've been wondering what you guys were going to do with the information you gathered from the PI.

Liv: Do you think it'll be best if your parents go with you?

Eros: The last time my mom tried to contact Callie, my sister was horrible with her. I want to speak with her first.

Liv: Good luck. I hope you can rebuild the relationship you guys had with her.

Eros: It'll be great if she can at least visit before Nyx has her baby.

Liv: That reminds me, have they come up with any names for the baby yet?

Eros: No. Nyx and Nate keep calling her blueberry.

Liv: I think that's sweet. April can't get here any sooner. You have to send me pictures of her.

Eros: I keep sending you pictures of everything I do. You never send me any.

Liv: I could send you pictures of my computer.

Eros: You said the other day that you were going to a bar.

Liv: To barre.

Eros: Ah, that makes more sense. For a moment I thought you started drinking too early. I can use a picture of you practicing.

Liv: Ha! Keep waiting for it, Mr. Brassard. :wink emoji:

Eros: A guy can always hope. Hey, can I text you back after the plane takes off?

Liv: You're already leaving for Boston?

Eros: Yes. I'm meeting Nate in New York, and we're flying to Boston tomorrow morning. I'll contact you soon.

EROS: Meet Nova Juliet Brassard.

Liv: Ooh, she's so pretty. Congratulations, Uncle Eros.

Liv: Wait, wasn't she supposed to be born next month?

Eros: She came a few weeks sooner. What can I say? The kid is as impatient as her mother. I should be running away from her.

Liv: You complain now, but she's going to have you wrapped around her little finger.

Eros: She already has. I love that sweet girl.

Liv: How is everyone?

Eros: Mom and baby are doing well.

Liv: I want to cuddle her.

Eros: *Fly to Seattle.*

Liv: *I wish I could. We signed a few new deals. I might be moving to Boston once Dad comes back to work.*

Eros: *Why?*

Liv: *We haven't found anyone to manage that branch. Instead of hiring someone, I'm going to take over while deciding what's best for the company.*

Eros: *I told you to merge the Northeast branches months ago. Am I going to say I told you so again?*

Liv: *No. We're doing it, but I have to figure out how to do it.*

Eros: *If you need help, I'm here.*

Liv: *Thank you. I'm not sure what I'd do without you.*

Eros: *Always a pleasure to help. Plus, you're handling everything really well. You just second guess your decisions.*

Liv: *Still, you keep me sane.*

Eros: *Hate to cut this short, but we're going to have dinner with Callie.*

Liv: *Callie is with you?*

Eros: *Yep. Nate convinced her to visit Nyx. So far, she has been friendly with us. I have hope that things are turning around for all the Brassards.*

Liv: *I'm happy for you.*

Eros: *TTYL*

EROS: *How's the new place? How is Boston?*

Liv: *The weather is nicer than in San Francisco during the summer. As I've told you, it gets colder during these months than during winter. Overall, the city is cute. I always wanted to live in a brownstone. Most women in rom-coms live in a brownstone. I might finally meet my soulmate.*

Eros: Name at least one movie.

Liv: You've Got Mail.

Eros: Oh, those types of buildings. So, you live in a glorified, costly apartment.

Liv: It's not a glorified apartment. It's a beautiful place. I have a view of Charles River. The best part is the private roof deck. You'd love the place. I take it that you watch rom-coms.

Eros: Of course, I do. As you know, I have sisters.

Eros: Three.

Liv: I wish I had at least one. Remember, I was excited about living close to Holly?

Eros: Yes.

Liv: She's planning on moving. They're still researching the best places for small families.

Eros: I'm sorry.

Liv: It happens. This relocation isn't permanent. Once we merge all the branches, I'm taking time off.

Eros: You keep saying that. You'll be a hundred by the time you finally buy a plane ticket to Hawaii.

Liv: Shut up. How's Persy feeling? I'm thrilled that you're going to be an uncle again.

Eros: She's doing well. She and Ford are excited. They just found out their spawn is going to be a girl. Mom is thrilled. It'll be like having Nyx and Persy 2.0. God, help me with these women.

Liv: That's adorable. Send me more pictures of Nova.

Eros: Nate and Nyx are in Seattle. I'll send you more when I go to visit them.

Liv: Hey, I'll text you later. Holly is here. We have a girls' night out!

Eros: Stay safe.

Liv: You should go out and party.

Eros: I'm heading to Costa Rica next week. There's a lot to do in the office this weekend.

Liv: Send me pictures of the farm. I'm so happy that things are working out for you.

Eros: You helped me a lot. I'll text tomorrow if I can.

EROS: Meet Leah Brooke Chadwick!

Liv: She's so cute—and looks a lot like Nova when she was a baby.

Eros: I didn't notice. You're right.

Liv: Congratulations, Uncle Eros.

Eros: It's Eos. According to Nova, the r is silent.

Liv: You're adorable as an uncle. Maybe it's time to get the wife and the kids. You'll be a great dad.

Eros: The business hasn't taken off yet.

Liv: It's doing great.

Eros: This is phase one. I need to make sure everything is working according to my plans before thinking about having a life.

Liv: Sounds like a new excuse to put your future on hold.

Eros: How about you?

Liv: I'm still in my twenties. That gives me a pass, doesn't it?

Eros: Not by much, but let's go with that.

Liv: I'm super happy about Leah. Though I wish to stick around, I have to sleep. Tomorrow is going to be long.

Eros: I forget you swear that Tuesdays are worse than Mondays.

Liv: They are.

Eros: Have a good night's sleep.

Liv: Same. x

Chapter Twenty

Olivia

I KNEW this was too good to be true. Dad always calls or texts before I go to bed with a laundry list of things he wants to be done before he wakes up. Tonight, he hasn't done it yet, until now. I should move back to San Francisco—or quit.

When I reach for the phone, I frown. It's Eros. He's supposed to be in Costa Rica.

> ***Eros:*** *Are you in town?*
>
> ***Liv:*** *Are we talking about Boston or Colorado?*

Eros: *Boston.*

Liv: *Yes, why?*

Eros: *Can I see you?*

I stare at my phone, check the time, and scroll up to read his last texts. He wasn't coming back from his trip until the end of April. Instead of answering, I call him.

"Hey," he answers.

"Where are you?"

"According to Google Maps, a few blocks from your house."

"A little late to ask if I'm at home," I joke, getting out of bed. "Of course, you can come to visit."

"Sorry, I know it's late, but I didn't know where else to go."

His voice is off. I wish I could understand what's happening, but instead of asking, I say, "I'll be waiting for you."

I change into a pair of leggings and a long sweater. I slide my feet into my flats and run downstairs. It's a good thing that the cleaning crew came today. The last time Dad and Dan came to visit, they hired someone to help me with my weekly house cleaning. It's hard to keep the place tidy when I spend most of the day at the office—sometimes even on weekends.

Dan is right. I'm becoming my father, and I don't even love what I do. All I want is to make sure that the company is working well so Dad doesn't have to worry about anything. As I approach the main entrance, I spot a car stopping by my place. A tall guy gets out of the passenger seat and shuts the door.

The driver helps him with his luggage. Eros walks toward me, shoulders slumped, his gaze fixated on the ground. *What happened?*

I open the door wide so he can enter. He sets the luggage on the floor and hugs me.

"Hey," I greet him, hugging him back. "Let's go upstairs."

He nods and follows me to the fourth floor where I live. After shutting the door behind him, I finally ask, "What happened?"

"Callie," he whispers. He sets his carry-on next to the coat rack, takes off his shoes, and puts his backpack on the bench I have next to the door.

"Is she okay?"

He shakes his head. Running a hand through his hair, he walks back and forth. "Last week, this guy, Isaac, calls me saying it's important that we speak." He stops, takes a deep breath, and stares at the ceiling. "Her husband. I had no idea she was married. We just saw her last March, when Nova was born."

I want to tell him that Nova is a year old. Persy's baby is almost three months old. I don't.

His relationship with Callie is fragile. If something happened to her, he'd be blaming himself for that.

"You know it takes me time to call back when I'm at the farm. This Sunday, Gil convinced me to go with him to the city. That's when my phone came to life. The texts and calls from my family began to roll in." He pauses, takes a deep breath. "Last Monday, there was an accident on the highway. A construction truck rammed against a bus."

He shuts his mouth and closes his eyes.

I know exactly what he's talking about. It was all over the news. There were no survivors. My heart stops. "She was there?"

He nods, turning to look at me. "I got in touch with Nate and Ford. They told me the funeral was on Friday. Of course, I couldn't leave town until today. I didn't know where to go. Colorado, where my family is or here to see... I'm too late to even say goodbye to her."

"I'm so sorry."

"You know what's the worst part?"

I stare at him expectantly.

"I still can't believe it happened. It's not sinking in that we lost her," he explains. "My parents are devastated. Nate told me that

Nyx isn't taking it well either. You know she always mothered Callie. Persy is coping better."

He holds his head with both hands and looks at the ceiling. I watch him as he takes several breaths.

"I hope you don't mind me being here," he says, finally looking at me. "After I landed, I took a cab and gave them your address. I'm sorry for coming unannounced. You're the only person I wanted to see."

I step closer to him, placing my hands on each side of his face. Our gazes lock. My heart hurts as pain radiates from his dark eyes. I want to take it away.

"Hey, I'm always here for you."

He slides a hand around the back of my head, bends closer, and hauls me in for a deep kiss. It's hard, almost ruthless. There's madness, pain, and need. I kiss him back, trying to soothe his soul. We devour each other with an intensity I've never experienced before. We feast. We ease the pain.

The bone-deep need for him increases as he grinds against me. We're jerking and pulling each other closer. My body aches. I'm not sure if it's his pain or a need to quench the thirst for him. We don't speak. I find the zipper of his jacket, slide it open, and shrug it off of him. He tugs at my sweater, yanking it off.

His mouth is now against my neck, traveling down my skin. Heat sizzles all over my body when he nips at my nipples. He kneads the other with his hand, fondling it. I cry with pleasure as he playfully bites my hardened beads. I can feel his warm breath against my bare skin. God, how I missed this. Him.

Eros's hands scoop under my ass, lifting me. "Where is your bedroom?"

"Down the hall," I answer, wrapping my legs around his waist.

"Stop me if you don't want me to continue."

"I want you," I mumble as I play with the lobe of his ear.

He places me on the edge of the bed, pulling my leggings off. "You were in pajamas, weren't you?"

I grin as I watch him push his jeans down along with his boxer briefs and kick them off.

"Wrap your legs around me," he orders. He grabs his length and presses it against my entrance.

"Condom," I remind him.

He frowns. "I'm clean. I haven't had sex since the last time we were together. How about you?"

"We're a pair, aren't we?" I shake my head. "Still on the pill. Well... I'm too busy to entertain the thought of going out with anyone."

"You need to stop working so much."

"Stop lecturing me and fuck me."

"Bossy," he whispers as his big, thick cock enters me deliciously slow.

His hands pin my wrists on either side of my head. There's no gentleness tonight. He kisses me as roughly as he thrusts inside me. It doesn't take long for me to come underneath him. We shudder and rock against each other while sparks fly out of my chest. As our gazes lock again, I see his soul bleeding and the rawness of his pain.

"What can I do for you?"

He gives me a sad smile. "Just be with me tonight."

I'm unsure of what to say or what to do. I kiss him, hoping that it's enough. That I'm enough for tonight.

Chapter Twenty-One

Olivia

THOUGH I'D LOVE to stay with Eros all day, my Tuesday is packed. I take a shower, get dressed, and leave a note next to the pot of coffee that's ready for him.

I'm at work. Call if you need me. Press the start button to get your morning Joe. In case you're wondering, it's the one you sent me last November. I'll try to be back around lunchtime. There's a set of house keys next to your backpack.

Liv

After a couple of video conferences with Dad and the team, I decide to leave the office for the day. Before I drive toward home, I text Eros.

Eros: *Where are you?*

Liv: *On my way home.*

Liv: *What do you want for lunch?*

Eros: *Are you playing hooky, Ms. Sierra?*

Liv: *Sort of. I'm bringing some work with me.*

Eros: *I'll cook for you.*

Liv: *I don't have much in my fridge.*

Eros: *You do now.*

Liv: *That's music to my ears. See you soon.*

When I enter my place, I yell, "Honey, I'm home."

"Lunch should be ready soon," he answers. "Get comfortable."

"I have work to do."

"You can do it afterward," he argues. "I promise to make it good for you."

"Promises, promises," I joke, heading to my room. When I pass the kitchen, I spot his shirtless back. Okay, I can take an extended break to see what this guy has planned for us. Since we're not going out, I put on a long cotton dress.

"What are you making?"

"Hey, beautiful," he greets me when I enter the kitchen. His lips brush against mine. I draw a deep inhale. We move toward each other, colliding. He pushes me against the wall, and I grab his bare shoulders. He crushes his lips to mine. It's a sizzling kiss. Deep. Passionate. Mad. I don't hold back. I never do with him. With us it's no longer just a kiss. It's a body and soul experience that pushes us to a different dimension.

He stops us.

"As much as I'd love to continue, we have to eat first."

I pout. "Since when does that matter?"

"You like your cheese sandwiches gooey," he answers, kissing my jaw. "I promise to make it up to you."

I graze his stubbly chin with my hand. "You're letting this grow?"

"You don't like my beard?"

"It's different."

"I usually let it grow while I'm in Costa Rica. When I go back to Colorado, I shave the hipster away from my face. That's what Persy and Nyx call it," he explains, grabbing my hand and pulling me toward the kitchen table.

"You already set the table," I say, impressed.

"After looking at your empty fridge, I assumed that you don't have many homemade meals," he says. "At least while I'm here, I plan to feed you."

"I might keep you longer than you intend to stay," I joke. "So, what have you been up to?"

"I visited Isaac." He clears his throat. "Whose actual name is Zack. I misunderstood his name. They married last November. It was a small ceremony with only friends and family. When I asked him why she didn't invite us..."

He takes a long deep breath, then he looks at me. "Our parents dragged us with them everywhere, but when Callie was born, they left her with our grandparents," he explains. "She didn't join us until she was much older. I never gave that a second thought. Except, it always made her feel like she wasn't really part of us. Nyx, Persy, and I are a tight unit. She's an outsider. Even though she loved our parents, she was ashamed of them. Inviting them was out of the question."

I clasp his hands.

"She never gave us a chance to be a part of her life." He squeezes his eyes. "We should've tried harder, and now it's too late. I can't even blame myself for not keeping an eye on her. She never allowed it. She always said, 'I'm not Nyx or Persy. Leave me alone.'"

"I wish I knew what to say."

He opens his eyes and looks at me. "Honestly, I don't need words. All I need now is to feel something other than pain."

This is something I know well. He's helped me forget and feel better twice. I sit on his lap, wrap my arms around his neck, and kiss him. I grind against his lap. His hand goes under the fabric of my dress. Moving aside my underwear, his finger touches my clit. One slides inside of me as his thumb works my clit.

"What happened to eat first, then play?"

"I'm thinking that I'll eat you first," he says, setting me on top of the table. "Lace panties. They're cute."

He slides them off and shoves them inside his jeans pocket. His mouth hovers right above the apex of my thighs. I forgot how good he is with his mouth and his fingers. In less than twenty-four hours, he has reminded me how good it is to have sex—with him.

It doesn't take long for me to cry his name and quiver. I hear the sound of a zipper opening. A moment later, he rams himself inside me. My legs are over his shoulders as he drives himself harder, rougher inside me. I love this side of Eros. His dark eyes glare at me with hunger.

There are never words when we're like this, together. Just lust and passion. Today I want to say, "I'm here for you. Take what you need. Let me heal your heart and your soul."

I bite my lip, muting the words. It'll be one of many unsaid phrases, sentences, and words between us. I keep them to myself, guarding them with my life.

There's no point in telling him anything. We're from two different worlds. We live separate lives. I have to be practical. I have to safeguard my heart.

As we both reach the peak and begin to shudder, he pulls me

toward him and holds me tight. So tight that we become one person. We share one heartbeat, one breath, and one body. The irrational-romantic part of my brain wants to stay like this for a long time. The rational part of my brain knows I need to move. This is too comfortable. I can fall into an abyss.

No one will notice my absence. I'll be lost forever.

If only life was fair and we could happen. Maybe in another life.

Chapter Twenty-Two

Olivia

EROS STAYS a couple of weeks in Boston. He spends his mornings hanging out with Zack, who owns a coffee shop. He's getting some kind of closure while trying to understand who Callie was. They're becoming friends. On Sunday, the words I've been dreading to hear since Eros arrived are finally spoken. "I'm leaving tomorrow."

We're in bed. This is the first Sunday I've taken off in a long time. I move on top of him and begin to rock my body back and forth.

"You think this is on-demand?" He smirks. "It's hard to keep up with you. No pun intended."

I giggle. "So, where are you going?"

"My first stop is to Colorado," he answers, giving me a sad smile. "Afterward, I'll go back to Costa Rica. I'm going to extend my trip for a month or two."

His penetrating gaze holds mine. I wish he didn't look at me like this. Like he could love me. Like I could be someone important to him. Like we could be something. Because I know we'll never be.

"Come with me," he offers.

"I will," I joke, reaching for his hardness and slipping it inside me. "After I ride you."

"Liv." He holds me in place. "I'm serious. Why don't you pack and come with me?"

Leaning closer to him, I whisper in his ear, "In another life."

While we lazily move our hips, I wonder if there's another dimension where we end up together or where we never meet. Maybe this friendship is beginning to get complicated for us, or just for me.

"Stop thinking, Liv," he orders.

He hates when I think while we're together. What would he say if he found out what I think of while we're together? He might laugh and call me a fool—a silly woman who still thinks like a girl.

As I begin to shake and quiver, he mumbles, "I wish you'd say yes. That you'll come with me."

If he wasn't mourning and trying to escape reality, I'd believe that he wants me with him. I know better. People say things they don't mean when they're in pain.

BY THE TIME JULY ARRIVES, Dad and I have finally merged the three East Coast branches into one. We acquired a building in Quincy, Massachusetts. Instead of paying an expensive lease in the middle of downtown Boston, we own a place where we can have all the employees from the DC, New York, and Boston branches.

Dad asks me to stay another year in Massachusetts. The same day I agree, Mom calls me. The doctor diagnosed her with stage 2 breast cancer. The news feels like a punch in the gut. Even though Canada has a great health system, I convince her to move to Boston so I can take care of her.

I find the best oncologist in Boston. Two weeks after she moves in with me, she's scheduled for surgery.

Eros: *I don't want to take this personally, but your one-word responses for the past month worry me. Are you okay?*

Eros: *Are WE okay?*

I choose not to answer. If I speak to anyone about what's happening with Mom, I might start crying, and I'll never stop. Dad knows about the diagnosis because Mom reached out to him too. She wants to make sure I'm taken care of if she doesn't make it. Every time Dad brings the subject up in our conversation or our texts, I stop him.

Once the doctor tells me that Mom is doing well, I'll break the silence.

Not answering the texts doesn't stop Eros from trying to reach me. He calls. Letting it go to voicemail doesn't work. I answered after the fifth attempt.

"Hello."

"Finally." He sighs. "What's going on, Livy?"

"What do you mean?" I play dumb.

"The last time I heard from you, you said your mom was sick," he states. "It's been almost three weeks. Since then, I only get monosyllabic answers from you."

"I'm not in a good place."

"No kidding." He sighs. "What's happening?"

"I'd rather not discuss this until she's in remission."

"Listen, I don't know much about the subject, but that can be years," he says, exhaling harshly.

"She's having a double mastectomy tomorrow," I say. "After that, she has a few rounds of radiation and chemotherapy."

"Are you in Canada?"

"No. I brought her to Boston with me."

"Good." He sighs, relieved.

My doorbell rings. "Hey, someone is at the door. I need to go. Can I call you later?"

"When is later?"

"I don't know," I say, as honestly as I can answer.

He hangs up the phone. If he's upset, I don't care. There are a million more important issues that need to be addressed before I worry about this call.

The doorbell rings again. I roll my eyes. The stupid intercom broke down last week, and the management company hasn't fixed it yet. It's probably Mom. She keeps forgetting the keys in the house. I should've gone with her to the mall, but she wanted to go alone. Perhaps because I would've paid for whatever she needed to buy.

When I reach the main entrance door, I do a double take. Through the glass, I spot Eros. He knocks on the window.

"You're here," I state as I swing the door open.

He takes me into his arms. "It's going to be okay," he assures me.

My throat has been clogged with tears since Mom gave me the news. I've been holding it together up until now. I begin sobbing. One moment I'm downstairs, and the next, we're on my couch. I let out everything I've been repressing. He mumbles soothing words. I'm not sure how long I stay in his embrace or when I fall asleep.

"Hey, sleepyhead, it's time for dinner." Eros's deep, husky voice wakes me up.

"You're not a dream," I mumble with a raspy voice.

"Did you rest?" He dusts kisses around my face.

I nod. "Thank you for... Why are you here?"

"You've been weird for the past few weeks. I put two and two together. On my way here, I decided to text because what if you weren't in town."

"Wait, did you say dinner?" I ask, worried about Mom.

He nods. "Your mom and I decided not to wake you up until dinner was ready."

"You met Mom?" I flinch.

"Yes, I met Beatriz. She's a lovely lady," he answers. "She's inquisitive, though."

"That's a nice way of calling her nosy."

He grins. "You haven't met my mother. Your mom is nothing compared to mine," he says as if warning me.

"So why were you avoiding me?"

I shake my head.

"Correct me if I'm wrong, but I think the lady was trying to handle this by herself," he states. "Why would you do that?"

"Saying it out loud makes it real." I almost choke. "Mom's sick. Do you know how many women die of breast cancer?"

I press the heel of my hands against my eyelids. I don't want to cry again.

"It's okay to cry," he mumbles, hugging me. "You're afraid to lose her. She's going to be fine, but I understand your fear. No one wants to lose a loved one."

"I'm trying to be strong for her," I sob.

"You're doing a great job," he says encouragingly. "She told me that you brought her to Boston within days of learning about her diagnosis. You got her the best care, and she's having surgery tomorrow. You're taking time off from work to look after her."

"It's the least I could do for her." I sniff.

"Sometimes, I feel like you don't like people to notice that you're a loving person." He presses a kiss on the top of my head. "Let's go have dinner. Tomorrow will be a long day. We need to rest. The next eight weeks are going to be daunting."

"You say it like you'll be here."

"I'm staying by your side."

Chapter Twenty-Three

Eros

LOOKING at Olivia's family life, I'm thankful for my crazy family. I can't fathom what it'd be like to have a sick parent and be alone in a waiting room. When my parents are sick, Nyx, Persy, and I look after them. Since Nate and Ford joined the family, they love and treat Mom and Dad as if they were their parents too.

For the past twenty-four hours, I've been tempted to ask her why she didn't reach out to me. I don't understand Liv. When my sisters need anything, they call me no matter the time of the day. I do the same. The day her father had a heart attack, it was the same. She called to cancel our dinner, not to ask me to be with her.

How can I make her understand that she can count on me? She's not alone.

"What are you thinking?" she asks.

"I wish I had been here for you from the beginning," I state.

"When are you heading next to Costa Rica?"

"Probably by the end of the year," I respond. "Everyone knows I'll be here for the next few weeks."

She tilts her head, giving me a strange look between confusion and delight. "You are?"

"I'd like to stay and make sure you and your Mom have someone helping out," I state. "This isn't going to be easy for either one of you. It's going to take some time for her to recover from surgery. Chemotherapy is draining for the patient and the family."

Liv rests her head on my shoulder. "I should say that you don't have to, but honestly, I feel a lot better now that you're around."

"I'll stay under one condition."

"That I don't steal your T-shirts?"

I chuckle. "No. That you call me the next time you need me."

She opens her mouth, then snaps it closed.

"You were about to tell me that you don't need me, weren't you?"

"I'm used to handling my parents on my own. When I was young, if Mom was sick, I had to take charge of the situation," she explains.

"You never reached out to your dad asking for help?"

She shakes her head slightly.

I don't know the relationship between her parents. Instead of saying something like, I'm sure your dad and Dan would be here for you if you asked, I kiss the top of her head.

"You know what you owe me?"

"Texts?"

I cup her cheeks, hold her face as I lean closer to her delicious lips. I capture her mouth, making the world disappear. It's only us for this moment.

Just for now, her mom isn't sick. My sister didn't die. The world is a place where we exist only for each other—at least when we kiss. This is the magic of Liv.

She makes me forget.

She gives me hope.

Today, I want to reciprocate. I hope that the next few weeks are less dreadful because I'm here, helping her.

When we pull apart, we're breathless. Her eyes have that shine I love to see when we're together.

"Hi," I say, giving her one last peck.

"That was unexpected," she whispers.

"I would've done it yesterday, but I waited for the right time."

"Is this the right time?"

I shrug. "No, but I couldn't wait any longer. I also have a complaint to file."

"Really?" She crooks an eyebrow. "The complaint department is closed until next year."

"I need to speak to a manager," I joke. "My first night at your house was different from the usual. If I had to rate my stay, I'd give it one star. *I was sent to the couch.*"

She laughs. "Mom is using the guest room."

I glare at her. "Who says I wanted to stay in the guest room? I always get to be in the main suite of the house"—I kiss her nose —"with you."

"If you behave, I might let you stay in there tonight."

"We're staying at the hospital for the next couple of nights," I remind her.

"You could—"

"We're taking turns, but you're going to rest one night. This is a marathon, not a sprint."

She smiles. "Thank you for being here for me."

"Always, Liv."

AFTER HER SURGERY, Beatriz spends two days in the hospital. Chemotherapy begins three weeks after the surgery. Liv and I get into a routine. I take care of the house chores while she drives her mom to doctor's appointments and chemo treatments and spends time with her. At night, we spend some time reading and then, when we go to her room, we spend a few hours having fun.

"Mom wants to go back home." Liv grunts, turning her face toward me.

God, I'm going to miss her when I leave. There's something about having these late-night chats after fucking that makes me feel connected to her. I wish I could stay longer. This week is going to be the shortest one in the history of the world.

"The doctor said three to six months of treatment. I don't know what to tell her without sounding like an authoritative parent," she says. "I just want her to get better. Why can't she let me look after her?"

"As a mom, she thinks it's her place to look after you," I explain. "It's normal for her to feel like she's been here for too long. I understand your point of view, but maybe you need to be a little more understanding about her feelings. She lost a lot in the past few weeks. My suggestion is to get her a counselor."

She looks at me and grins. "I wish I knew your sister. She'd love to hear you say that."

I pull her closer to my body and kiss her nose. "I trust that you'll never tell her."

"We can look for a counselor. But how do I explain to her that it'd be best if she stays?"

"This might be a discussion she should have with her doctor before she makes a decision," I suggest. "It's his place to tell her that she can't just pack and leave without finishing her treatment."

"That's doable. I'm not sure what I'm going to do after you leave," she whispers the last three words.

It'd be easy to answer, "The same thing I did when Callie died. We live our lives in these parallel universes where we meet for only a few beats." Those moments are never enough. It pained me to lose my sister. It fucking killed me to leave Liv behind. But that's what we do every time we see each other. We absorb as much as we can from the other person and we move on. If only I could convince Liv to come with me. This isn't the first time that I'm dreading the moment when we have to go our separate ways.

There's nothing I can do or say that will change the outcome. This is probably the way our relationship works. She says that there's always a reason why you meet someone. Maybe we met so when we face our worst storms, we'll have each other to hold on to. In this moment I could tell her, "Every time you fall asleep, you'll find me in your dreams."

It's sweet, corny, but unrealistic. We're too old to believe in pipe dreams.

Maybe all I wish is that she wouldn't look at me the way she does all the time, like she could love me.

Or it's probably a reflection of what my heart is trying to avoid, falling for the impossible.

There's a saying, do as I say, not as I do. So I move on top of her, pushing her legs open, and drive inside her. "We promised not to talk about it until Sunday night. I'll talk to Persy tomorrow to see if she knows a good counselor for your mom."

She bites her lip and nods. Does she feel the same as I do? Not that it matters. There's nothing we can do. Only a lot of shit unsaid between us that feels like it's eating me alive.

Persy would have a field day if I ever tell her about Liv. Not that I can explain my situation. What can I tell her? See, there's this girl —now woman—I met long ago. She's fantastic. Things between us are great when we're together. She'll glare at me. I'll say something like, "No, listen. We live in some dimension where we can coexist as one."

She'll definitely snort when I end with, "The issue is when the real world calls us. We have to go our separate ways."

Persy would dedicate a few podcasts to discussing the insanity that's Liv and me. She might even get a book deal out of my pathetic life.

Sometimes I wonder what would happen if I say, "Fine. If you don't want to come with me, I'm staying."

Not that I can stay. I live part-time in Colorado. The other part I travel, finding new suppliers, or working at the farm in Costa Rica.

"You're the one thinking now." She lifts her hand and smooths my forehead.

"I wish I could stay longer," I confess.

"In another life," she says, like always.

It sucks that in this life we are just two strangers who happen to come across each other when the wind blows the right way. It's useless to wonder which reality I should be in when I already know where I belong.

"WHO IS THIS FRIEND?" Persy inquires.

"Obviously, you don't know her," I answer. "As I explained, she lives in Boston."

"I can send you a couple of names," she sighs. "They work like me, virtually. It won't matter where she lives."

"Thank you. I owe you one."

"When are you coming home?" she asks.

"Why?"

"Everyone is out of town. Ford and I need a date night. I'd love it if you could babysit Leah."

"I should be back next week. Where's Nyx?"

"She's going to be in Seattle until my birthday," she answers. "Ford sent our parents to South Asia—all expenses paid. They won't be back until mid-October."

"How are they doing?"

My parents are struggling just as we are. They lost their baby. The kid who never accepted them. It's to no one's surprise that they feel as if they've failed Callie.

"Better," she whispers. "It still feels unreal. One moment we had hopes that things would turn around between us. The next we received the call—Callie is gone. As a parent, you're not supposed to bury your child. I think we're all doing the best we can to grieve, to come to terms with how things ended between us, and most importantly to understand that none of this was our fault."

I close my eyes, pinching the bridge of my nose. It feels as if we lost her twice. The first time was when she moved away because she couldn't live with us. The second was when she died. We can't get real closure. I understand that we were a lot different, but how the fuck did we end up like the bad guys in her story?

"The hardest part is moving on without blaming myself for what happened to her," I confess.

"I said it then, and I'll repeat it: We weren't driving that truck. The accident could've happened here in Colorado, and still, it wouldn't be our fault. We hurt, and the pain makes us take some of the blame."

"I'm working on it," I mumble.

"If it makes you feel any better, you're the best brother a little sister can have."

"I'm lucky to have you and Nyx."

"So, where are you?"

I chuckle. "In Boston."

"Helping your friend?"

"Yes. As I said, I should be back home next week. Text me the information when you gather it, okay?"

There's a loud wail on the other side of the line. "Go, your boss is getting grumpy. Give her a big kiss from her favorite uncle."

"I will. Please, take care of yourself."

"You too."

Even when I'm here helping Liv with her mom, I wonder if I also came to take a break from the ghosts. The past. From all the noise rattling inside my head. All the chaos that unleashed after Callie died. For some unknown reason, I can breathe a lot better when I'm with Liv. If I could, I'd stay until Beatriz is better. I smile, recalling Liv's words, "In another life."

Chapter Twenty-Four

LIV: Leah is adorable!

Liv: *Thank you for sending all those pictures. Are you on babysitting duty?*

Eros: *That took a long time. I thought you were ignoring me again.*

Liv: *Mom had her last chemo treatment. They're running another set of tests afterward to decide if they're doing radiation treatments too.*

Eros: *How is Beatriz doing?*

Liv: *The therapist helped, but she still wants to go home as soon as the doctor allows it.*

Eros: *How are you?*

Liv: *Concerned. I'm afraid that she'll relapse.*

Eros: *Because you won't be able to watch over her?*

Liv: *I know it's an unfounded fear, but I can't help myself.*

Eros: *You should try going to a therapist too.*

Liv: *Are you going to one?*

Eros: *As a matter of fact, I am.*

Liv: *I'll think about it. So, what have you been up to?*

Eros: *The pictures I just sent you are from yesterday. I spent the entire day at Persy's babysitting Leah. Apparently, I'm her official nanny.*

Liv: *You spend a lot of time with her.*

Eros: *She's fun to be around. Plus, I can bring my computer and work from here.*

Liv: *I take it you're visiting Persy.*

Eros: *Yes. She and Ford have a couple of deadlines to meet. I offered to help. It's a cool deal. I get free food while working. the best part is that I hang out and play with my favorite girl.*

Eros: *When are you going back to work?*

Liv: *The last week of October. It'll be good to go back to normal.*

Eros: *You miss bossing people around.*

Liv: *I might. It's fun.*

Eros: *Hey, Leah is crying from the top of her lungs. It's time to change her diaper and get her ready before Persy feeds her.*

Liv: *Good luck!*

EROS: *Happy Thanksgiving!*

Liv: *Happy Thanksgiving to you too.*

Eros: *Where are you celebrating?*

Liv: *In Boston. Dad and Dan arrived last Monday. They're pampering me.*

Liv: *Well, Dan is pampering me. Dad is micromanaging me.*

Eros: *Where's Beatriz?*

Liv: *Mom left for Canada last week.*

Eros: *Are you okay with that?*

Liv: *I'm handling it well enough. Where are you spending the day?*

Eros: *We're in Seattle at Nyx's house. Christmas is at my parents' and for New Year's we're going on vacation. They haven't told me where we're going yet. As long as it's warm and tropical, I won't complain.*

Liv: *I should propose that to Dad and Dan. Boston is too cold.*

Eros: *How long are you going to stay there? i thought you'd be leaving the branch once you found someone to manage it.*

Liv: *Probably another year. After that, I have no idea what I'm going to do.*

Eros: *I can hire you.*

Liv: *We agreed that it'll happen when I can buy half of the company.*

Eros: *Hurry up, lady. The company's value is increasing as we speak.*

Liv: *You have no idea how happy I am that it's a success.*

Eros: *Thanks to you. this is your brain child.*

Liv: *It's ours. I'm glad you took a leap of faith. If I had kept the idea, it'd be an afterthought.*

Liv: *Hey, let's text later tonight or tomorrow. I need to start peeling the apples for the salad. Happy Thanksgiving.*

EROS: Happy Groundhog Day!

Liv: You're not funny.

Eros: What does it mean if you see your shadow? Another successful year. Six weeks of bad luck, or six months of good luck.

Liv: Hey, at least my birthday isn't some distress call.

Eros: Happy birthday, Livy! I hope this is the best year of your life.

Liv: Thank you. Also, thank you for the care package.

Eros: I thought coffee, bracelets and candy were better than flowers.

Liv: I love everything, even the birthday card. I am not that old. Always remember, you're older than me, Grandpa. Where are you?

Eros: I'm still in Costa Rica, finalizing a few details for the new distillery. Later today, I'm flying to Quito.

Liv: You're a busy man.

Eros: It's all about the hustle. Did I tell you that I have enough money to buy out my silent investors?

Liv: That's great.

Eros: Gil wants to buy ten percent.

Liv: I heard that there's only one season left of his show. He's retiring. Does that have anything to do with your company?

Eros: As a matter of fact, no. He met a guy.

Liv: It's never too late to find your soulmate.

Eros: I knew you'd say that.

Liv: I'm glad he's happy.

Eros: Hey, I'm heading to my last meeting. I'll text you later tonight. Happy Birthday, groundhog.

Liv: Thank you?

EROS: Can you believe Nova is two years old?

Liv: She's so cute. I love her dress. (I secretly want one),

Liv: How's the party?

Eros: If I were a kid, I'd love it.

Liv: Is that code for I want to get out of here?

Eros: Yes. Not only because there are like a million toddlers screaming. My sisters introduced me to "a friend."

Liv: Ha! What happened to the last one?

Eros: Mimi?

Liv: No, there was someone after her. Colette?

Eros: Would it sound bad if I say that I lost track of them? I can't remember their names or faces.

Liv: Tell your sisters to stop setting you up with the entire state of Colorado.

Eros: I already did. According to them, I'm too old to keep my string of one-night stands.

Liv: How long is that string?

Eros: Let me think... the last time I had sex was late August.

Liv: Seven months ago?

Eros: Yep.

Liv: You were with me then.

Eros: I know. I've only slept with you in the past few years.

Liv: Why do they think you are sleeping around?

Eros: They assume. I don't correct them.

Liv: Do they know about me?

Eros: Do you want them to know?

Liv: You're close to them, and yet, there are things they don't know about you. That is weird.

Eros: I could tell them, but the implications might rupture the space-time continuum. Think about the consequences. You'd have to move to Colorado with me.

Liv: You're diverting the conversation.

Eros: *If I tell them about you, they won't let the subject go until they meet you. They are relentless.*

Liv: *Well, then let them set you up with every woman in the world. Maybe they'll find you a wife.*

Eros: *I doubt it. They have bad taste in women.*

Liv: *If you ever need a blind date, I have a few friends who might want to give you a try.*

Eros: *Har har.*

Liv: *Did I tell you I hired Calvin? He's going to head the branch in Colorado.*

Eros: *Who is Calvin?*

Liv: *He's Holly's husband.*

Eros: *Didn't he have a job here?*

Liv: *He did, but they let him go. Their options are to find a new job or go back to San Francisco and live with her parents. So, I offered him the job.*

Eros: *I can't believe your friend has been here for a year, and I haven't met her yet.*

Liv: *If I go to visit her, I'll introduce you two.*

Eros: *If you ever come to visit, I'll call that a miracle.*

Eros: *Hey, I need to leave. It's cake time.*

Liv: *Send me more pics.*

Eros: *I'll do it.*

EROS: *They set me up with a stalker.*

Liv: *Another blind date?*

Eros: *This one is worse than the others. She is a stalker.*

Liv: *You're exaggerating. If she keeps calling or texting, just block her number. Every time a telemarketer calls or texts, I block them. If someone weird texts, I block the number. It's easy.*

Eros: This is different. She actually got my personal address, my company address, and my private number.

Liv: Are you serious?

Eros: I found her earlier outside my house, waiting for me. She wants to know when we're going on a second date. She also wants me to meet her parents.

Liv: Wow. I'm sorry.

Eros: Not as sorry as I am. I told her that we're not going out again. Let's hope that's the end of it.

720-5XX-XXXX: Hey, hottie. Text me.

LIV: Happy Thanksgiving!

LIV: Merry Christmas!

LIV: Happy New Year?

LIV: Are you okay?

LIV: What's with the radio silence?

———

LIV: I'd go and visit you, but I don't have your address.

———

LIV: Okay, I'm taking this as some kind of code for fuck off, Liv.

———

LIV: I can't believe it? After all these years, I deserve a fucking goodbye.

Chapter Twenty-Five

Olivia

"I'M DONE UNPACKING!" I call my fathers once I set the last empty card box in the garage.

"That was fast," Dan says. "Unless you shoved half of the boxes into a closet."

"They're in the basement," I admit.

Moving isn't as fun as many presume. I'm thankful that Dad convinced me to hire a moving company. They packed everything for me. The real work began when I arrived at my new place. It's been a week since I opened the first box. Yep, it took me a week to put everything I need for now away. The rest can stay tightly packed downstair.

"When do you start your new job?" Dad asks.

"This Friday, but if you need anything, call me," I assure Dad. "Mondays are my free days. I can always work at night—"

"Liv, everything is going to be fine. Holly needs you, and you need to take a break," Dan assures me.

"I would if your husband wasn't so stubborn."

Dan clears his throat. "He knows his limits."

"Well, as I said, I'll drop by the offices twice a week to check in," I promise.

"It's not necessary," Dad argues. "I've run this company since before you were born. Nothing will happen if you take a few months off, sweetheart."

This trip isn't exactly time off. Holly is pregnant with her first child. She was on bed rest during the holidays. The doctor ordered rest and zero stress for the next six months. She can't just take time off. Her event planning business is on the rise. I offered my help.

How hard can it be to organize parties and weddings?

I'm sure it's like project management but with tulle, ribbon, and flowers instead of wood, nails, and blueprints.

Helping my best friend and her spawn comes with a price, though. I'm leaving Dad to run the company by himself. What if he has another heart attack because he can't take a chill pill and he loses track of time easily?

"You say that now, but—"

"Let's compromise," he says. "You run your weekly meeting with all the branch managers. We do our weekly call every Friday."

I sigh. "Fine. Please, just promise me that you won't overdo it. The last thing we need is another visit to the hospital."

"I'll be watching him, Liv," Dan says. "Why don't you relax too? After this, we're all taking a long vacation."

"Maybe," I say vaguely.

"What are your plans for today?"

The doorbell rings. "Holly is here. We're having lunch, and she's going to walk me through a day in the life of an event planner. I'll call you tonight."

"YOU'RE HERE!" Holly says as I open the door.

"I am." I hug her. "Look at you, all beautiful and glowing."

She smiles. "Wait until I start showing. Then, I'm going to look like a shiny snake who ate a mouse."

I roll my eyes. "Exaggerating much?"

"I'm serious. Everyone says that their boobs grow, their hips widen... I'm still flat as a pancake." She fondles herself.

"Should I leave you alone?" I point toward the staircase. "There's a guest room if you want some privacy."

She looks around the house. "This is pretty. Why did you choose a house instead of an apartment?"

"Unlike my apartment in Boston, there aren't any places here with an upstairs terrace—unless I leased a penthouse. After discussing it with Dad, buying a house was the best choice. It's an investment. I can set up a garden like the one I had in Boston, plus there's a patio."

"If I'm lucky, you'll stay for a long time," she says excitedly.

"Unlikely, but I'll have a place in Colorado. When I come to visit you and the spawn, I won't have to worry about hotels, Airbnbs, or sleeping in my car."

"There's always a couch in my house." She gives me a tight smile and begins to nibble her thumb. She has that habit of biting her nails or the skin on the side when she's nervous.

"What's wrong?"

"Calvin is worried about his job security," she says.

"Why? Is there something happening in the branch that he hasn't reported?"

"No, but you're here. Why would you need him?" She takes a deep breath after speaking too fast.

"I'm helping you, not him. I'll be in and out of the branch just to check on everyone—not just him," I explain to her. "Once you're ready to go back to work, I'm taking some—"

"Let me guess." She interrupts me. "Some time off to think about what you want to do with your life?"

I burst into laughter. "Dan said the same."

The excuse about my father being sick is too old to use anymore. I guess after so many years, I learned to love the company. The people who work for me are no longer employees but family. Taking over the company wouldn't be a hazard, but is it really what I'm meant to be doing?

I'll always have that question if I don't try something new.

"Who knows? I might enjoy planning parties," I joke.

"Though I'd love to hear you'll stay in Colorado, I know that's not going to be the case. Once I come back from maternity leave, I suggest you take a few weeks off before heading back to work for your dad."

"I'd rather not discuss that. Why don't you train me for the job of a lifetime?" I clap, excited. "I get to tame bridezillas for the next six months."

"Lesson number one, you have to be nice to them." She glances around and whispers, "Even when you want to slam their heads against the wall."

"Noted. Don't kill any clients." I pretend to type on my phone.

"Lesson number two, never sleep with the best man or the fiancé."

"Well, now you're just mean. What if he's super hot?" I challenge her. "You'll take away the opportunity of a lifetime just because you have rules."

"That's how I lost my partner," she reminds me. "I can't have you running away with some guy and leaving me stranded."

"Fine. Just remember I sacrificed my happily ever after for your child. You'll be indebted to me forever. You might have to give me your firstborn." I wink at her.

She laughs. "I'm happy to hear that you're still dramatic enough to entertain me. I'm so glad you came to Colorado."

Me too, except I thought I'd be able to see someone else while I was here, but he stopped talking to me. It's been two months since I stopped hearing from Eros. I have no idea if I offended him or if he just decided that our friendship wasn't worth it. Next time serendipity brings him back into my life, he's going to be carrying a baby and holding the hand of a beautiful woman—his wife.

My heart twitches slightly.

I ignore it.

We don't care about *him*. He's nobody to me.

Nobody.

Chapter Twenty-Six

Eros

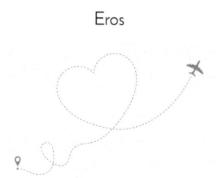

"FUCK," I groan as my phone blares "Girl on Fire."

I cover my eyes with one arm and let it go to voicemail. It must be Nyx calling about some family issue, an appointment I might've forgotten, or just to nag me about my personal life. When we were children, she appointed herself as my personal life coach. Not that I needed one.

Do I fuck up sometimes? Yes. Just like everyone else in the world.

For some reason, she believes I can't function without her ordering me around. Someone has to set the record straight and remind her that I'm the oldest of the Brassard siblings. Also, at almost thirty-six, I can buy my own clothes, put one foot in front of the other, and run a successful business.

She should worry about her three-year-old daughter and the little one that's on the way. Not me.

I'm sure you think *that someone should be you*. I could set the record straight, but I can't. While she's pregnant, she gets a bit too emotional. Her husband will try to kick my ass. I like Nate well enough not to get into a fight with him.

After a couple of minutes, my phone rings again. This time it's the tune "Confident." That's Persy's ringtone. I'm going to change their ringtones to something more dreadful, like "The Imperial March," or as some like to call it, Darth Vader's theme song.

I scrub my face with both hands because it's evident that my sisters have some kind of emergency. There's a second option; they found me the perfect woman. It's been their mission to find me a bride. I adore my sisters, but their meddling is out of control.

Do I feel alone?

Yes. Should I start thinking about settling? I'm working on it. It's something I can do on my own. They don't need to intervene.

Sending this call to voicemail would only delay the inevitable. I take a swig of water from the nightstand next to the bed. I clear my throat to make me sound awake. When I look at the time on my phone, I moan. It's too early.

"Yeah?" I try to sound calm, but my voice comes out growly. Persy is the one who jumps to the conclusion. "Who peed in your coffee?"

"Seriously, Persy?" Nyx protests.

"Great, I have not one, but the two annoying sisters on the line,"

I complain. "Do either one of you realize it's too fucking early in the morning?"

"It's seven your time," Nyx responds.

"Ah, the lady isn't in town," I say mockingly. "Where in the world are you?"

Nyx is one of the best lawyers I know. Her law firm has offices in Oregon, New York, Seattle, and Colorado. She works mostly from home—wherever she's at. Nate, her husband, has offices in New York, Colorado, and Seattle. They jump from one house to the other without a pattern. Other times, they stay a month or more in another country.

They plan on doing so while their children are young, not that they have many children. There are Nova and the new groin demon on board who, in my opinion, doesn't count yet. The point is that Nate wants them to have the same life we did while growing up.

I doubt he can compare the life he plans on giving to his children with ours. Mom and Dad are archeologists. They traveled around the world to some of the oldest, most interesting sites. When we were young, they dragged us with them.

We never spent a weekend at a resort, a vacation home, or some luxury Airbnb. Our accommodations were modest. There were times when I'd share a room with my sisters. To this day I hate bunk beds—or sharing a room with someone else. Well, except for Liv, who has offered me shelter in her bed for the night. For that, I'm always willing and available.

The point is, traveling around the world so their kids can learn about other cultures, see the wonders of the world, and learn other languages is a lot different from our childhood. My sister should set her husband straight. Maybe I'm off, and he's aware of our youth. I don't have complaints about it. I loved every minute of it, but it was a lot different than he assumes.

"We're still in New York," she answers with a chirpy voice.

"You're two hours ahead of me," I protest. "Can you have mercy on me?"

"I've been up since five arranging everything for our trip to Denver," she argues.

"What's your excuse, Persephone?"

"Leah woke up at six?" Persy yawns.

Before I can argue that she's lying, Nyx laughs. "I woke her up a few minutes ago."

Leah, her daughter and one of the most adorable toddlers in the world, loves to sleep. I swear that kid was sleeping all night long before she was a month old, unlike my other niece, Nova.

That kid screamed bloody murder all night until she was six months old. I know because, along with Persy and my parents, we took turns watching her so Nate and Nyx could have some time to sleep.

"It's Sunday." I think. "Is there any way you can call me in a couple of hours?"

"It's actually Saturday," Nyx corrects me. "Were you partying last night?"

I could remind them that I've been in Costa Rica for the past three months building houses. This could be the right time to remind them that I stopped partying years before they did. I desist from discussing nonsense with these two. If I want to move this call along and catch a couple more hours of sleep, I have to cut to the chase.

"How are you planning on torturing me?"

They laugh. No matter how old they are, some things will never change with them. These two are like twins. I'm the poor big brother who has to keep up with them. I love them, but they can be a nuisance.

"The next time you need a babysitter, I'll remind you of this call," I threaten them. "If your second spawn is as demanding as you, Nyx, I'll make sure to disappear for six months."

"Aw, Eros is a little sensitive this morning," Persy teases me.

"Again, why are you calling me?"

"We're going to be in Colorado for the next couple of months," Nyx states. "Last night, I was on the phone with my friend—"

I groan. I knew this was going to be some kind of setup.

"No!"

"You haven't let me tell you about—"

"The answer is still *no*," I interrupt her again. "I need you to stop setting me up with your friends, colleagues, or clients."

"But she's—"

"Or someone you met while having dinner with your husband who reminded you of me," I pause, "Like crazy Ariana."

She wasn't just the worst blind date in my life. Nyx met her while shopping for baby clothes. She didn't even know her well enough. My sister gave her my number. I had to change it... and sell my house.

"I have a restraining order against her."

"That was Persy," Nyx defends herself.

"It's all the same."

"We're helping you find the love of your life. As far as I can tell, you're still pining for Misty," Persy states. "That's unhealthy."

They have no idea what unhealthy is. For years I've been enamored with a woman who might be a figment of my imagination. Liv. The blackhole her absence created sucks another piece of my soul.

What happened with her?

"It's too early to have a conversation with you two." I claim.

Now, Misty is a subject I don't like to discuss. She's been my friend since college. We're close. In fact, when I moved from New York to Colorado, she decided to do the same.

Is she the person I'm meant to be with? I don't know. The question came up when Richard fucking James Prince III came into the picture.

Yeah, he is as ridiculous as his name. He's not a Prince, though his family is one of the richest in the state. That is, of course, if we don't count my brothers-in-law's wealth or mine. But that's now, and not then. Back when they got engaged, I couldn't offer her much.

I had just launched my business. How could I say, "Hey, be with me instead of that asshole," when all I had was a house with an upside-down mortgage.

Then there's Olivia and the millions of unanswered questions and conversations we never had. The silence we clawed to keep what we had alive. If we ever had anything.

Liv's theory about soulmates doesn't fit. I'm almost sure it's not real. When you're meant to be with someone, destiny assembles everything so that you can make things happen. Things with Live never worked; with Misty...the jury is deliberating.

Her wedding with prince got cancelled. Their relationship became a roller coaster. This could be the perfect moment for me to swoop in and say, "We make sense. Let's give this a chance."

My sisters are not on board with my plan. They have many different theories on why I'm so obsessed with Misty.

Persy says it's because I'm lonely and maybe broken-hearted.

I'm not sure where she gets the broken-hearted part, and obsessed is not the right word. Fixated sounds like I'm a stalker too. There has to be a word that doesn't sound eerie. Pining sounds like a teenager crushing on his hot teacher.

"Can I at least tell you my plan before you shut it down?" Nyx offers.

I sigh. While Nyx speaks, I mute the call. I place the phone on my nightstand. Knowing my sisters, I have enough time to pee, brush my teeth, and put on my workout clothes before they are done talking.

"What do you think?" Nyx asks when I pick up the phone.

That I'm glad I missed your plan.

This is the best moment to feign anger. "Remember when you were single, Nyx?"

"What's your point?"

"You hated going on blind dates," I remind her. "I do too."

"At least I tried."

Phew, I guessed right. She wants to set me up with some friend of hers.

"We don't want you to end up alone," Persy takes over the conversation. "It's going to be a casual dinner among friends. Life is short. Misty is not the answer. She feels comfortable. You need—"

"I don't need counseling, Persy," I warn her.

This is a lost battle. Two against one isn't fair. Nyx is a great litigator. Persy is a psychologist who specializes in couples counseling. People email her, listen to her podcast, and read her books, hoping that they'll find love or fix their broken relationships.

I'm just one tired as fuck without ammunition to battle against them.

"It's okay to be happy," she continues. "How many times do I have to tell you to go to counseling? Grieve, and let it go."

And now we're going to fixate that I refuse to be happy because Callie died. They swear something happened to me after her death that makes me not want to date anyone.

Nothing happened.

I went to counseling.

I'm fine.

"I have a busy schedule. Why don't we reschedule this intervention for when hell freezes over?"

"Eros." Persy's annoyed voice is the last word I hear before hanging up the phone.

If only they knew that today I'm having a long overdue conversation with Misty after her appointment. We're discussing our future. She has to end her on, off, on again relationship with Prince. I should've asked her what this appointment is all about that she's dragging me to. I hope it's not another mani-pedi. I do a lot of things for her, but I refuse to be her shopping-spa-antique picking buddy.

Chapter Twenty-Seven

Olivia

"IT'S OVER, OLIVIA."

"Listen, Kelly," I lower my voice so my other clients won't hear my conversation. "This is what we spoke about when you hired the company. There are moments when you feel overwhelmed. It can be a lot. We're here to help you so you can enjoy the journey that's organizing your wedding. Connor is the love of your life."

"Is he?" She sniffs. "What if there's another man? What if I fell in love years ago and I let him go? What if I haven't met my soulmate?"

A degree in philosophy would've come in handy with this job. Her questions are too deep, even when they sound like a severe case of cold feet. These brides are worse than my father when one of our suppliers doesn't deliver on time. I think he trained me well for this moment. He just didn't know it.

"Close your eyes, Kelly," I prompt her. "Think about the day you met Connor. The first moment when he left you breathless. Remember the day when he asked you to be his lifetime companion? You said yes. It was one of the happiest moments of your life. Among all the people in the world, you chose each other to walk through this difficult journey called life."

All I hear are sniffs on the other side of the line. I continue, "This is a good time to approach him, hold his hand and say, 'I need to lean on you for support. I need us to remember why we're taking this step.'"

"You're right, I love him. His mother—"

"She's trying her best to stay away, but it's hard because her only son is starting his own family. She's becoming an outsider," I explain. "This is your moment. I understand why this is frustrating and overwhelming. We will figure out ways for her to feel included. That doesn't mean she'll take over the organization of the event. This is all for you and Connor. I'm the gatekeeper. I need you to trust me."

Listen, sweetheart, if I could keep my father away from his company for more than a year, I can take this woman down too.

"Thank you." She sniffs.

"Anytime. I'm here for you."

When I hang up, I stare at the phone, wondering if I did the right thing. Her questions were logical. If she has doubts, maybe she should go to counseling before saying I do.

It's none of your business.

But it is. What if this was me?

At what age do we fall in love?

What is love?

Do we all have a soulmate? If he was the love of my life, would I care how his parents are?

Everyone has a different theory. A simple Internet search will back me up. When it comes to love, no one answer fits all.

I was ten when I fell in love with Levy Cross. He broke my heart two weeks later. Jane Stevens had pretty black hair, and her mom sent cookies in her lunch box.

I was fourteen when I met Ron Garner. Within three weeks of me leaving Canada, he found another girl who wouldn't be away too often and for too long. The last two years of high school, I stayed with Mom. Those were the only two years I was able to have a somehow normal adolescence. Pierre Gagnon and I were an item during our senior year. We broke up before winter break because I was moving away to attend university in the United States.

It wasn't much of a choice but a matter of going to Dad's alma mater.

There's Eros. Even though we were somehow stranded, we spent the most intense, glorious, fun day and a half of my life.

It didn't make sense—we didn't make sense.

He lived in New York City. I lived in Elora, Canada. He was in grad school. I was just graduating from high school.

He had a ten-year plan where he'd be rich, have a beautiful wife, and a gorgeous family. I hadn't chosen a college yet.

That should've been the end of us.

It wasn't.

Serendipity brought us together again and again. We were text buddies. The occasional call kind of friends. I don't want to think we were fuck buddies, but sometimes it feels like it if I'm honest with myself.

Tall, dark, handsome Eros was a sexy dream.

He is definitely not the one for me. Sometimes, I have these fantasies where he sees me and says, "It's always been you, Liv. I love you forever."

I'm not in love with the guy. It's just the feelings he stirs when he's around that got to me, like a high from some aphrodisiac or a drug. For one reason or another, I can't seem to meet *the perfect guy*.

Needless to say, I'm thirty-one, single, and considering a mail-order groom from England. Someone like Benedict Cumberbatch, Tom Hardy, or even Jude Law (but with hair).

Love is real.

I know it. I've witnessed it for the past three months.

I live vicariously through my clients.

One of my favorite moments during the ceremony is when the groom watches the bride walk toward him. There's no one and nothing else more important in the world for him but the woman who's about to promise him forever.

My least favorite part is the father and daughter dance. I even try to pick the song I'll play for us when it's time for Dad and me to dance. Who knows... at this pace, I'll never get a wedding of my own. This is why I enjoy doing what I do, the moments when I help the groom and the bride create the event of their dreams.

Sighing, I walk back toward the table where the bride and groom taste the different cakes, fillings, and frostings that we recommend according to what they like.

I look at the trays George, the baker and owner of the place, set on the table. The one marked as *Loved* is empty.

"Do we have any favorites so far?"

"This is it. Don't you think, Pablo?" Laura Moy asks her fiancé. She points at one that is placed on the *Don't Like* tray.

Okay, I'm guessing they didn't understand the instructions. Is the *Maybe* tray the one that holds the flavors they disliked? Yikes, why is it so hard for people to follow simple instructions?

Pablo nods. He grabs another piece of the cake.

I look at the tag under the small cake. Pulling my tablet, I scribble all the details. Then I read it out loud to confirm I got everything right. "We're ordering a cake for two hundred and fifty guests. Pink champagne cake with white chocolate mousse filling and raspberry buttercream frosting?"

"Can you add two hundred and fifty cupcakes to go?" Laura requests. "It'd be a fabulous party favor, don't you think, Pablo?"

No, but it's your wedding.

My job is to guide, suggest, and find what they need. I can't tell them what not to do.

Am I on the verge of telling them that their lavish wedding could feed an entire town in Africa? Eros could use that money to back up some small businesses in Ecuador. I shut up because we can't lose this client. Also, Eros isn't part of my life anymore. He cut me off without any explanation—the asshole.

"Whatever the lady orders," Pablo answers.

I smile and hand them the tablet. "Initial here, here, and here. Sign at the bottom that the information is correct. Sign next to the total price for the cake. We will send you the bill this Monday. I don't need to remind you that food, flowers, and printing material invoices are due upon receipt. None of the items are refundable. The price tag for today also includes the bridal shower cake, the delivery fee to the event, and the groom's cake."

I take a deep breath after I finish my speech. As I told Holly, this disclaimer sounds like I'm reading the small font of a shady contract. Not that I've ever hired a wedding planner before, but I'm sure that everyone requires a fifty percent deposit, and they ask for the final payment at the end of the event.

Laura claps, giving me a coy look. I smile back. Pablo's groom's cake is a lot better than the wedding cake. Maybe it's just my geeky personality thinking that a Lord of the Rings themed cake for a wedding is fantastic.

"Our next appointment is on Friday," I confirm with them.

"You're a lifesaver, Olivia," Laura says as they leave the bakery.

Her compliment is good enough but not fulfilling. I'd rather work for Dad.

Chapter Twenty-Eight

Olivia

AFTER I PLACE the cake order with George, I drive back to the office for my one o'clock appointment. This job isn't what I ambitioned when Holly asked me to help her for six months or so. Coordinating lavish parties for wealthy people sounded enticing. Not that I would've turned her down. Our friendship has endured time, tragedy, and distance. She's the closest thing I have to a sister. Three months after I arrived, I'm ready to move back to San Francisco.

My phone rings. Holly's name appears on my dashboard. I touch the green button and say, "What's new, boss?"

"Your one o'clock is here."

"Are you at the office?"

"Maybe?"

"Why did you hire me if you're going to be working every single day?" I try to sound like an angry mother chiding her child. "What is the point of moving across the country if you're going to do whatever you want?"

"San Francisco isn't across the country." She makes a sound between a chuckle and a groan. "Plus, next weekend is the babymoon."

"Pardon my ignorance, but what's a babymoon? Are you sacrificing something to the moon so the baby will be born healthy? Or is it a sacrifice to Poseidon since you're going to be by the ocean?" I laugh.

"There you go again, giving me a hard time about the baby."

"I can't help myself. And it's not the baby, but your weird rituals. There's the gender reveal, the babymoon, and the diaper shower, which I shouldn't confuse with the baby shower. You could call the babymoon a vacation before the baby is born. Nope, there has to be some weird name to it," I pause, clearing my throat before I say, "I'm judging you. Now, what were you calling me about?"

"As I said, your one o'clock is here," she repeats. "Judge me as much as you like. It gives me a pass for when I judge you."

Holly and I are more like sisters sometimes. She knows me a lot better than I know myself. I dare to say the same about her. Then again, I might be wrong, and Calvin, her husband, is the one who knows her best.

"The Wilfred-Brown consultation?" I confirm because Debbie, the receptionist, overlapped appointments yesterday, and it was a disaster.

"Yep," she corroborates. Her tone is strange. I'm not sure if she's concerned or just tense. That's her permanent state of mind. Everything is urgent and due yesterday. She's one of those people who sets her clocks fifteen minutes ahead so she's never late. She scribbles her deadlines daily so she won't miss them. She has a to-do list to create a to-do list.

"Hol, don't stress out. I should be there in five minutes," I assure her, pushing the gas pedal.

"I'm fine," she assures me. "They came in early. I just wanted to give you a heads-up. Debbie walked them to the conference room and offered them some refreshments. She's leaving for the day."

I sigh. "Remind me, is this a full-service wedding or just the basics?"

"It's an initial consultation," she says. I hear her pressing the keys of her keyboard. "You're not going to love this. They canceled their wedding a couple of years ago. One of them is high maintenance."

"Which one?"

"I don't know. They weren't my clients. This was when Jessy and I started the company before she sold me her half and left."

Right, the friend I never met who married a client and left her stranded with an angry bride, a growing business, and considerable debt. "Ugh."

"You're great at handling our special cases," she says optimistically. "I'd love it if you can sell them the full service. We could use the extra money for a down payment on a house."

I laugh. "If you need money, I can lend it to you."

"That's kind of you, but you know what they say about friendships and loans."

"No, I don't. The offer is on the table for you to take it," I suggest. "Can you tell me anything about the couple?"

"He's so hot!"

I chuckle. Since she started the second trimester of her pregnancy, every groom that crosses her business threshold is the most gorgeous man alive.

"Does Calvin know that you crush on all your clients?"

"This isn't the pregnancy hormones, Liv," she assures me. "The guy is smoking hot. Imagine if Rodrigo Santoro and Diego Luna had a child who grew up to be the most gorgeous, sexy, super-hot man alive."

"Yet another reason to leave your husband," I joke.

"And lose a client?" She snorts. "Never. I'll just take a picture and add it to the hottie grooms's album."

She ends the conversation before I can remind her that I am in charge. She should be at home resting and enjoying her free time before the spawn arrives.

It takes me almost ten minutes to reach the office. Since it's nearly one, I head to the conference room. I wiggle the handle of the conference room and push the door open. I hate to be unprepared for my meetings. I hate even more the sight of the groom.

Holly was right. He's handsome. When I enter, he unfolds his tall figure from the chair. His shirt stretches along his broad shoulders. The thin fabric allows me to see every ridge between his muscles. I can even remember his tattoos.

I'm unprepared for the thundering of my heart inside my chest.

I loathe the uncontrollable need to jump into his arms. Under different circumstances, I would even kiss him. Then I'd say, "Where have you been? I can't believe that you ghosted me. What did I do to you?"

Now, I understand why he disappeared. He's getting married.

I despise that the groom is the man who makes my axis spin recklessly. That we spent one of the best nights of my life together when I was eighteen. He made me feel whole every time we were together. For some inexplicable reason, I feel as if he's taking everything he once gifted me back.

He's snatching the bits of hope I carried with me. Who knew I had them?

"Olivia," he greets me, and his thousand megawatt smile brightens the room.

I want to remind him it's Liv. Not Olivia. That's what my clients, strangers, and employees call me. Not my friends. I guess we're just acquaintances.

"Hi, um..." I'm not sure if I should address him as Mr. Brown or Mr. Wilfred. Damn it. If I had read the freaking file, I would've known what to expect. Isn't his last name Brassard? Did he lie to me?

No, he's Persy Brassard's brother. Unless that's a pen name.

His facial expression changes to a more solemn one, and he prompts, "It's Eros."

I wave my hand. "I knew that. I just couldn't remember your last name," I answer with a snippy tone.

Planting a big smile on my face, I extend my hand toward the bride. "Hi, I'm Olivia Sierra."

"Misty Wilfred," his fiancée responds.

The name Misty sounds familiar. Where did I hear that name before?

She's gorgeous. Tall, slim with glossy blond hair. She could be a run away model. They are an attractive couple. Eros, he is an easygoing guy. So, she must be the high maintenance one of the two. As soon as she learns that there was something between her fiancé and me, she'll fire us.

Misty arches an eyebrow and asks, "So, you two know each other?"

Chapter Twenty-Nine

Eros

LIFE ISN'T FAIR.

I learned a long time ago that life is like a poker game. Destiny deals the cards, and it's up to us to figure out what to do with them. You can bluff and play to win, or fold and live in misery. I choose the former. There are times things work out in my favor. Some others, I keep faking it until I make it. I learned this from my family.

My parents are the definition of optimistic. They say that we learn to prepare lemonade and enjoy what life throws at us or watch the lemons rot. Mom and Dad are big believers in enjoying what we have instead of yearning for what we can't reach.

It's incredible how they handle life, love, and loss. Callie's death was hard for everyone, but especially for them. A parent should never have to bury their child. Even though it was tough, they're still going. I look up to them. Though at times they drive me crazy—like my sisters—the way they live is incredible.

Mom always insists that I should seize the day. It drives her crazy that I will jump out of an airplane, but I plan every detail and take my time to make any moves when it comes to my future. It's pretty simple. I had it all once, invested it in a business that didn't work out, and lost everything. Since then, I have stopped being impulsive when it comes to my professional life.

I guess she doesn't remember when I left my profitable job in New York, moved to Colorado, and lost all my savings. Those years when I would invest in anything that looked shiny and gainful. Businesses that would end up making me look like a stupid opportunistic man-child. Nyx, my sister, told me that once. She might've been slightly right. I signed contracts without reading them thoroughly. I lost time, money, and credibility.

Those mistakes are experiences. Lessons I used to create a new and better life. A future where I can see more than just getting out of debt and paying my mortgage. Now, I can think about having a family.

You know what is also unfair? Relationships. I can't make them work for me. And here, in the same room, I have exhibit A and exhibit B.

Liv stopped talking to me. Since I was in Costa Rica, there wasn't much I could do until I came back home. Instead of flying to Denver, I took a detour to Boston. She doesn't live there anymore. I knew she was thinking about moving, but she never told me where.

Of all the places in the world, she's here—in my backyard.

Seeing that whatever we never had was over, I called Misty. I finally decided to stop listening to my sisters and do something with our future. She couldn't do lunch with me but agreed to grab a cup of coffee after her meeting. I'm still wondering why she asked me to be a part of this freaking meeting—pretending to be her fiancé. Or what was I thinking when I accepted? It's probably because she just asked me to do it when we stepped into the elevator.

This is so fucked up. Faking in front of Olivia doesn't feel comfortable, it feels wrong. Not that she cares. She has been ignoring me for months. She couldn't even remember my fucking name.

If I had to choose between them, I... I don't want to be in that position. Liv is... special.

But Misty is the woman you should spend the rest of your life with, idiot. You're trying to fix the oversights from your past.

For all you know, Olivia might be with someone. I glance at her finger. I relax when I don't see a ring on her hand. Who knows, maybe she found the man of her dreams and that's why she stopped talking to me. That's why she's here. She moved for him and not for me.

Life sucks, love sucks, and I'm fucking doomed.

When Callie died, Misty and her fiancé had broken up too. That could've been a great time to swoop in. It wasn't. Those were some of the darkest days of my life. Liv was the one who made things less grim when I needed it the most. I couldn't think of being with anyone but Liv.

She wouldn't come with me, but she did for someone else.

My love life is a fucking joke. I'm tempted to pinch myself to make sure this isn't a nightmare. Because fuck, look at where I stand. I'm between the woman who makes certain moments brilliant or less dreadful and the one who has been by my side a third of my life.

This isn't a love triangle. It's me having another fucking moment of realization that relationships never work for me.

Why are we even here?

The whole, just go along with me sounded great up until Olivia crossed the threshold. I don't want to lie to her. I'm terrible at lying. Though, since when did she become a wedding planner? And how the fuck did she forget my name? I remember her clearly screaming it the last time we were together. This would be a good time to drag her into another room and remind her who I am.

Damn it. Why am I so worked up about this?

"It's good to see you, Olivia," I say casually, because the last thing I want is for Misty to know about our strange relationship.

She smiles and nods. "What can our company do for you?"

I frown. Seriously, she doesn't know me?

"Well, we're getting married." Misty wiggles her big ass diamond in Olivia's face.

She's the last person that would be impressed by that rock. She'd actually say something like, "Do you know how many people you could feed with that?"

Liv gives me a disapproving glare.

"I'd love to have a big wedding," Misty continues. "We're looking for just the right event planning company."

"Well, we plan events. You came to the right place," Olivia answers. The snark in her words is too light for Misty to notice, but I know it well.

"We want a January wedding. My mother thinks I should give her at least eighteen months."

Olivia's eyes stare at the ceiling while her fingers touch her thumb one by one. Then she looks at us and smiles. "January is a slow month for weddings. I'm sure we can make it happen. Is there a theme you're looking for? Winter Wonderland, New Year—"

"It's a wedding," Misty snaps at her.

Olivia waves her hand. "I'm wondering about the colors, flowers, and general decorations. Though, in countries like Canada, we have weddings with themes. In any case, we integrate your favorite flowers, colors, or something significant for the two of you. Maybe January is the month when you started dating or met."

Misty chuckles. "We met during the summer. It was hot and humid. I had never been to New York City before. Eros was kind enough to show me around."

"So, you've been together for a long time." Olivia smiles. This time it's a tight gesture.

"Since freshman year of college," Misty informs her.

Olivia grips the pen she holds tightly. She glares at me. "You and Misty have been together since college. College sweethearts, that's so romantic. Imagine, someone being faithful to you since your late teens." She looks at Misty. "You're a lucky woman."

"I know." Misty, who doesn't understand Liv's tone, smiles.

Olivia glares at me. "You're a prize. Let me go for our binder so I can show you some of the events we've organized."

I'm frozen by her hateful glare. Liv is loving. She's not like this. Fuck, I want to tell her that this isn't true. I'd never do anything to hurt her. Ever.

When she closes the door behind her, I turn my attention to Misty. "Why did you tell her that we've been dating since college? Why are we here?"

"As I said, I'm shopping around. They can't know the groom is Richard."

"Because...?" I frown when I realize what she just said. "You are back with him?"

Before she could answer, Olivia enters the room. "I'm sorry. It seems like the other consultant is using it. We could reschedule you for next week. I'm booked, but I'm sure we can fit you in with someone else."

Misty huffs. "You came highly recommended. They said you're the best in town. *The wedding wizard.*"

"You must be talking about Holly."

"No, I was at a wedding a couple of weeks back. I saw you."

Should I tell her that her *wizard* runs a construction company?

Nothing against Olivia. The woman is brilliant at what she does or plans, but what the fuck is she doing here? I doubt she'll be here for our fake wedding. Her father might need her. If not, her mom. Everyone else is more important to her. She puts others first rather than change her plans and do something that might make her happy.

Olivia takes a deep breath and says, "I could show you some of the pictures from the most recent events."

"That would be lovely."

I tune them out while they look at the pictures. I'm sure most grooms don't give a shit about what's going to happen during the ceremony or what they'll eat. I have other serious problems in my hands. Misty is planning on marrying that asshole. That's not even my issue. She just told Olivia that I'm a fucking cheater—and a liar.

This feels like one of those dreams when I arrive at the class-room naked and unprepared for a test.

I should text my sisters or my brothers-in-law. There has to be a way to wake up or get out of this mess.

Eros: *I saw Olivia.*

Persy: *Who?*

Nyx: *Airport girl.*

Nate: *Who the fuck is airport girl?*

Ford: *I thought you were declaring your undying love to Misty.*

Persy: *Langford Chadwick, I told you not to support that behavior.*

Nate: *Aw, Ford is in the doghouse.*

Eros: *I am... I was. It'll happen after we're done with the bridal consultation.*

Persy: *Who is getting married?*

Eros: *It seems like Misty and Prince asshole are back together, and the wedding is a go too.*

Ford: *Abort. She's back with him. You're too late and too slow.*

Nate: *And that is coming from the late bloomer. Back away, buddy, and look somewhere else.*

Persy: *She's not the woman of your dreams. If she was, you'd have noticed her EIGHTEEN YEARS AGO!*

Nyx: *I agree with Persy.*

Nate: *Who is airport girl?*

"What do you think, Eros?"

I look up. Misty and Olivia stare at me expectantly.

I blink twice. Shit, I wasn't paying attention at all. "About?"

"We were discussing the caterer and some of the suppliers," Misty responds. "I mentioned you might be able to provide some organic and sustainable products."

"It depends on what you're looking for." I pause, staring at my phone.

Olivia knows what I produce better than anyone. I don't understand why we're having this conversation. I'm not marrying Misty. I should tell her that, and then what?

Nyx: *A girl he met while stranded at the airport. They have the most romantic history.*

Persy: *Is she getting married too?*

Nate: *Wow, you know how to choose them. :ROFL emoji:*

"Personally, I'm not looking for anything. If you want your products to be included during your wedding, you can contact the owner. She'll let you know about our policies," Olivia says, and I loathe the business tone.

What happened to my fun, playful girl? Why the owner and not her?

"When can we start organizing the event?" Misty, the woman who is only shopping around, asks.

"Once you decide, call the receptionist with your dates. If we're still available, we'll send you our contract. After that, Debbie will create a timeline and suggest some dates for your first meeting."

"Let me discuss this with my fiancé, and we'll get back to you early next week."

"Of course." She places her business card in front of Misty. "There's my email. You can reach me through my direct line, or you can call Debbie."

There's a knock on the door. Holly, the owner and who I now assume is her best friend, enters the room. Why didn't I put two and two together? Probably because there are a lot of Hollys in Colorado and the world.

"Sorry to interrupt, Liv, but your two o'clock is in the waiting room."

"Perfect timing," Olivia smiles and shakes Misty's hand. "If you have any questions, don't hesitate to call me."

She glares at me. "Congratulations."

Chapter Thirty

Olivia

MISTY GRABS EROS'S hand as they walk outside the conference room. Any other day, I'd walk them to the door and chat about their plans for the day. I'd try to remind them that I'm here to help. I can't. All I want to say is, "Your fiancé is a cheating bastard. While you've been together, he's slept with at least one other woman—*me*."

Should I check myself for STDs? The guy swore I was the only one in years. I'm so gullible I believed him.

The eighteen-year-old who had a massive crush on Eros is

crying. All the memories of us shatter and fall to the floor. The first moment I saw him. Our time at the airport. His offer to go home with him because I didn't have any place to stay for the night. The first kiss we shared.

"Do you want to share with the class?"

I shake my head.

"Something happened there. I heard the 'fucking bastard' scream coming from the bathroom," she insists. "If you don't want us to take this job, we won't. I'm not going to let anyone treat you poorly, no matter who recommended us to them."

I arch an eyebrow. "She claimed to be at a wedding I organized a couple of weekends ago."

Holly nods. "Plus, the Prince family gave her my personal number."

"The who?"

"They're one of the richest, oldest families in Denver."

"I thought you didn't have socialites, like the New Yorkers."

"We don't," she confirms. "But there are a few families that hold some power when it comes to social events."

"Well, I won't be here in January when they have their big event. She can waltz hand in hand with her fucking fiancé toward the sunset. I refuse to witness that."

"What did he do?"

"Remember Eros?"

She smirks. "Your imaginary, hot, sexy boyfriend from Canada?"

I roll my eyes. "He is real. I never claimed him to be my anything," I state and clarify the facts, "He's American. I'm the one who is Canadian. Canadian-American."

"Sorry, but every time you see him"—she draws air quotes—"and tell me what you guys talk about and do, it sounds surreal."

I tilt my head toward the door. "That's him."

Her eyes open wide. She points at the door. "Him?"

I nod once.

"You slept with that... hunk?" she stutters.

"Several times." I pause. "While he dated his college sweet-heart." That sentence smothers my memories with mud and filth. I feel dirty.

I. Am. The. Other. Woman.

"He was my first," I whisper.

"Somewhere in hell, there's a special place for people like him," she concludes. "We won't take that wedding."

"You need the money."

"We have rules," she reminds me. "We can't be emotionally involved with the bride or the groom. You slept with him. I hate him."

I don't think that's a real rule, but this is why I love Holly. She's the most loyal friend in the world. I feel pathetic. How stupid was I to believe all his lies? I doubt everything he told me since we met. That fun family that traveled all over the world while growing up. He made me want to visit other countries.

"Well, I just got closure," I state. "If I ever thought we'd hook up again or have a coffee together, I won't do it."

"You know how you can forget about the bitter taste of this encounter?" I give her a questioning look. "Let me set you up with—"

"Seriously, Holly?"

"Hear me out," she insists.

"I have work to do. You need to head home to rest," I order.

Ever since I moved to Denver, she's been trying to set me up with her friends, neighbors, or her husband's friends. I don't want to be with just anyone. I'm not ready to find the man of my dreams. "I'm over men and Eros Brassard—or is it Brown?"

Holly turns around and speeds up toward her office. "Did you say his name was Eros?"

"Yes," I repeat, catching up with her. "I thought his last name was Brassard. He lied about it too."

"Fucking asshole!" The thunk sound on her desk makes me jolt.

When I enter her office, she's staring at the screen of her computer. "His name is Taylor Brown."

I shake my head, walk around the desk, and read the information. It reads Misty Wilfred and Taylor Brown. "This is wrong. I had no idea what to call him. He reminded me that his name is Eros. His fiancée didn't correct him."

I wrack my brain trying to remember if I ever heard him mention the last name Brown—or the name Taylor.

"Something doesn't add up," she states, taking back the folder and dialing the phone. "The number they gave us goes to a sandwich place."

"Didn't we call to remind them about this meeting?"

She shakes her head. "No. She called yesterday to set up the meeting. I remember because Debbie and I were on our way out. She called me on my phone. You were at the Silas event."

"We never give a last-minute appointment. Can you check the caller ID for her number?"

"They were recommended by the Prince family," she states while looking at her phone. "No. It was an unknown number. I had to give her an appointment. No one mentions the name Lorna Prince casually."

"Who is Lorna?"

"The wife of the late Richard Prince. He died like five years ago, leaving his estate to his five children. Three scorching guys. His daughters are gorgeous. We've organized several events for them, including the wedding of her oldest daughter."

"So, one of the most powerful women in society's name is mentioned, and you jump?"

"It's business, Liv." She nods. "I knew you were available and just booked her. They wanted you."

"Are you sure we're not taking it?" I repeat.

"If Lorna calls, I'll just tell her the groom is a fucking cheater."

"If this woman is so important, why didn't you place a reminder call?"

"We believed it was unnecessary. They were coming the next day."

This upsets me even more. I'm raging. Can I cancel my dinner with her and her husband's friends?

I want to buy two dozen cronuts and binge-watch *Schitt's Creek*. The second option is heading to visit my bestie and drinking a bottle of tequila with her. That's a no since she can't drink—or stay up too late. Plus, she has that stupid dinner with her friends.

This is definitely another reason for me to pack and leave.

"You can make it for another few months, can't you?"

Holly knows me too well.

"I said I'd be here for you. Once the baby is ready to rub your feet, I'll leave," I joke.

"Olivia."

"I'm fine."

"You're hurt," she insists. "When this happens, you like to escape."

She's confusing me with Mom, who tends to move on to a new house, a new town, or a new country after a breakup or a divorce. So, I don't have a plan on what to do next. It's because of the circumstances. First, it was my parents exchanging me every year. Then, it was college, grad school, work... Just when I thought I might be settling in San Francisco, here I am, in Colorado helping her.

"He's nothing to me, okay. My pride is bruised." I shrug one shoulder and give her a tight smile. "Ultimately, I'm not the one marrying a cheater."

"Just don't pack and leave without telling me," she requests. "At least call if you need to talk to me."

I stare at the frame she has on her desk. It's a collage with pictures of her wedding day, her puppy, and her husband. Another one of them in front of their current place. It's the image of someone who figured out her life at an early age and followed her dreams.

"You'll get my call, even if it's after midnight. I promise. Now, turn off the computer and head home."

"We'll see you tonight, right?"

I nod.

I head to pick up my stuff and leave. I don't have time to deal with men or Eros Brown's memory—or whatever his real name is.

Chapter Thirty-One

Eros

I'M USUALLY A LAID-BACK PERSON. Seriously, I don't give fucks about anything. I don't care what people think about me, except a few: my family, friends, and Olivia Evelyn Sierra.

Seeing Olivia's face while we were leaving ignites something unfamiliar. Misty grabbing my hand feels all wrong. I snatch it away from her.

"What was that?" I ask, poking the elevator button.

Her smile appears. "We're trying to get the best wedding

planner in town to organize *my wedding*. I wish you had stuck with the plan. You're supposed to be Taylor Brown."

"Olivia and I know each other," I state, trying to control my anger.

We step into the elevator.

"It's a small favor. I've done a lot for you."

"Was I supposed to fake amnesia?"

She tilts her head to one side. "She barely remembered you or your name. I think your ego is bruised. That's why you're upset."

This has nothing to do with my ego. It's Olivia who I'm concerned about. The air crackles around us when we're close. This time it wasn't because of the chemistry we share. The moment Misty said we've been dating since freshman year of college, the atmosphere changed. The sizzle was pure rage.

She thinks I'm a fucking cheater. That I slept with her while I had a girlfriend. I told her once that I don't lie. Yet, here I am, looking like the biggest fucking liar.

"You caught me off guard," I argue. "Why didn't you bring your fiancé with you?"

She shoots me a defiant look. "Why do I feel like you and the wedding planner have a history?"

"We met a few years ago. I happen to come across her from time to time," I explain loosely.

Olivia is hard to define. I'm not just talking about our relationship. She's complicated in her own way. God, I want to go back and explain to her that everything that Misty said was a big fat lie. I've never been with Misty—I'm not sure if she's going to believe me.

"It doesn't matter. I just want to make sure she's the right person for me. I'm not impressed, though. It felt like she wanted us out of the room."

"So, explain to me how you are going to justify my presence when you hire them?"

She sighs. "This might get messy."

"It could've been simple. Why the charade?"

"I want to make sure they're going to treat me right no matter who I am," she states. "Being Richard Prince's fiancée is weird. I bet if she knew who I am, she'd have treated me like a princess. It's hard to be part of that family. You never know who is friendly because of your position and who is a friend."

Yes, if she didn't think I'm a fucking cheater, she'd have been nicer to you.

This could be the moment when I tell her that Richard is not the man for her. I should just sit her down now and get everything off my chest before she continues with this charade. But what is it that I want to tell her? That I'm fucking angry because she hurt Liv.

"If being with him is such a problem, why are you back with him?"

"I love Richard."

"He's not going to stop being Richard Prince," I remind her. "You'll become Misty Prince. Your kids will be part of the family that everyone judges."

"Once we're married, things will be different," she states.

"You should talk to Persy about this," I suggest. "It sounds like you want to marry, but you have different expectations."

She huffs. "We're not discussing that part of my relationship. What do you know about love? You can't even commit to a paper clip."

"I don't use paper clips—or paper. Go green. It saves trees."

That's all I say because she's slightly right. I have never committed to anyone. It's not the lack of wanting but my shitty luck. Liv never wanted more than those moments we happened to coincide in the same space. What was I supposed to do? The one time I tried to move on—well, here we are.

"The bottom line is that we're getting married. My mother-in-law wants the best for her son. It's obvious that I have to hire them."

"Again, why didn't you bring *him*?"

She rolls her eyes. "It's complicated. What do you think?"

That you're making a mistake. "When did you and Prince get back together?"

"You're going to think it is too corny," she answers, tapping her phone and smiling.

"I have an extremely corny sister who gives cheesy advice to whoever listens to her podcast," I remind her as we get into the car.

"How is Persy doing?" she asks, putting on her seatbelt.

I start the engine, turn my attention toward her for a moment, and state, "You're changing the subject."

"I'm asking because last night you mentioned she's having morning sickness."

Misty is a nice person. I don't say that lightly. There's a reason why she's my friend. The way she behaved with Olivia was strange. Someone could even address it as bitchy. Nothing like the Misty I've known for years.

"No, that's Nyx," I correct her, going along with the conversation and adding, "Would you like to have some coffee?"

"Right, you have something to discuss with me." She sighs.

Honestly, I don't know if I want to talk to her—ever again. I'm baffled by her behavior. The fury running through my veins is making me shake. She's unaware of what she did to Liv. I've never hurt a woman, but I swear I want to open the door and push her out of the car. I don't. And she did all this because she wants to marry a man who doesn't fit in her life.

"While I drive toward downtown, why don't you tell me about your corny and gleeful life?"

"You're going to think I'm stupid," she insists.

I do, but that's beside the point.

"Misty," I press.

"It was a week before Valentine's Day."

"You've been back together for more than a month?"

"About," she answers casually.

"Why am I just finding out about it?" My voice sounds confused, not angry.

This entire situation should upset me because I have plans for us. It doesn't. I'm angry because she blindsided me, and we lied to Olivia. Mainly the latter. I have this urgency to take the next exit, call a car to take Misty home, and go back to clarify everything to Liv. Which is weird. I never give out explanations, not even to my parents. If I did something wrong, bring on the punishment. Sometimes I took the blame for my sisters. Someone had to look after them.

"You've been in Costa Rica since January," she answers.

"Working," I say defensively. "There's a position in the company open for you. If you wanted, you could travel with me."

She chuckles. "I'd rather sleep in my own bed. Tents and sleeping bags aren't my thing."

"You're diverting the conversation—again."

"He called me on New Year's Day," she starts. "This time, we restarted things slowly. Phone conversations, flowers, and the next thing you know, we went out on a date. We've been talking about our first breakup and why things never work out every time we try to get back together."

"I don't understand why the sudden need to organize a wedding when you're *patching* up your relationship."

She sighs. "I knew you wouldn't understand it."

"Try me."

"We were on a break. His mother was sick. His family needed him. He didn't want me involved because everything was too much for him. The bottom line is that he loves me." I don't think I've ever heard her speak so fast and without taking a breath between sentences.

"But do you love him?"

"I do, with all my heart. I wish you could be a little more supportive," she presses.

"There's a reason why you two broke up. If Mom or Dad were sick, I'd want the person I love with me. Why get back together?" I counteract.

"Please, I thought you'd understand him. You're like him."

"I'm not."

"You went missing for over a week when Callie died," she fires back. "Maybe it's a guy thing."

"What's a guy thing?" I ask, sounding genuinely perplexed by her suggestion. I'm buying myself some time. How dare she compare me with Richard fucking Prince? I wasn't missing.

"It seems like men hide or reject those who love them when they're hurting," she states. "Not that you ever get hurt. Where were you when Callie died?"

I open my mouth and then close it. I don't have an answer. When my baby sister died, I was angry, lost, and hurt. Each one of us has a role in the family. Mine is to make sure my sisters are always safe. I failed Calliope, my sisters, and my parents. I spent that time with Olivia. She put me back together and breathed some life in me. I didn't want to be with anyone but her.

"Exactly, you hid from everyone. If it were me, I would have been with my parents or Richard. The people I love."

This is a discussion I refuse to have with her. My sisters are annoying but also lifesavers. When my phone begins to ring, I answer immediately, "What's happening, Persy?"

"Can you pick up the N family?"

I chuckle and wonder if Nate and Nyx will choose a name that starts with an N for baby number two. I hope they do because it's kind of fun to call them the Ns. "I thought they were in New York."

"If you had let us finish our conversation, we would've told you that she was on her way to Denver," she says, annoyed. "I texted you, but you haven't responded yet."

"At what time are they landing?"

"Twenty minutes," she answers.

"Listen, I'm close to their house. Let me drop Misty off, and I'll switch cars."

"Hey, Misty." Persy sounds so chirpy, you'd think she's her best friend. "I hope you don't mind that we're interrupting your day."

"We were actually done," Misty answers. "You guys have fun."

"You too," Persy answers, ending the conversation.

"I guess the conversation will have to wait for another day," she states.

"Sorry, I had no idea they were coming in today."

"Do you keep in touch with them when you're out of town?"

"Always," I respond. "I just don't keep track of their where-abouts when I'm in Costa Rica. It doesn't make any difference to me, as long as they call at decent hours."

"Maybe that's your problem," she states.

"My sisters are annoying, but never a problem." My voice booms inside the car.

When I exit the highway, I sigh with relief. Misty's apartment isn't too far from Nyx's place. I can't continue having this conversation with her. I have to arrive at the airport right about now.

"No, I mean that you don't have a life because you dedicate all your free time to your family."

As I park in front of the building where she lives, I look at her and say, "You, of all people, know the deal with my family. We're close. My sisters are my best friends. After almost four years of knowing my brothers-in-law, I could say they fall into the same category. I have a life."

She gives me a dismissive glare and scrunches her nose. "It's weird."

"I'm not sure if you're complaining, judging me, or... What are you saying?"

She shrugs. "You say I'm your best friend, but I haven't heard from you in months. You'd rather hang out with your sisters than go out and find a girlfriend."

"I'm too old for hookups," I state. "You kept telling me that for years."

"You listened to me a little too late," she says, getting out of the car and closing the door, more like slamming it.

If I had time, I'd go down to figure out what's bothering her. I can't. Nate's plane is landing soon, and I don't want them to wait. After that, I have to find Liv. We need to straighten things out because she deserves better than the lies she heard today.

Chapter Thirty-Two

Eros

WHEN I ARRIVE at Nyx's place, I spot Persy's SUV. Instead of going down, I text Nate.

Eros: *Do you need me to pick you up, or are THEY staging an intervention?*

Nate: *We needed you to pick us up, but we assumed it wasn't happening. You were with Misty. Ford picked us up.*

Nate: *That's why they are staging the intervention.*

Eros: *They're staging an intervention because I couldn't pick you up?*

Nate: *No, they are doing it because you're obsessed with Misty.*

Eros: *I wouldn't call it an obsession.*

Nate: *That's between you and your sisters. You leave us out of it. I told you to leave it alone.*

Eros: *I like your twin better.*

Nate: *You say that now, but when you need my plane, all I hear is, you're my favorite brother-in-law.*

Eros: *Can I borrow your plane to go to China?*

Nate: *You have nowhere to run. Those two will catch you.*

I jolt when someone knocks on my window. It's Persy.

I turn off the engine, unbuckle my seatbelt, and leave the car.

"You're back!" Persy embraces me, and I hug her back.

"It's good to see you, but what happened to we never lie to each other?" I point at the house. "They're already here. I'm killing myself to make it on time."

"Your tone of voice told me you weren't alone," she states. "You'd be mad if I had said, 'Hey, we want to talk to you about this Misty issue.'"

I laugh. "According to her, you are my issue."

Persy frowns and crosses her arms. "Interesting. She sees your family as your problem. I wonder if she's projecting herself."

My sister, the psychologist, is pretty chill. She doesn't over-analyze shit, but there are exceptions to her usual behavior. I can see her asking me more about my conversation with Misty. I'll have to describe the tone of voice we used, the exact words, and what led us to that moment. She's going to call me often so we can go through Misty's words until she comes up with a satisfactory answer that proves Misty's statement wrong.

She doesn't need to spend days thinking about this nonsense. I'm aware that my sisters aren't my problem. They're annoying, but I wouldn't have them any other way. Their husbands might say I'm the problem since Persy and Nyx pause their lives to organize ridiculous interventions. They expect me to stop my reckless behavior, learn, and grow.

Since I'm going to endure a couple of hours with them pointing out how my love life is a disaster, I plan on giving them a hard time too.

"You know she's right, Persephone," I claim. "I could be going on with my Saturday. Instead, I interrupt everything to follow your fake instructions."

"You could've said no."

"Where are my girls?" I ignore her, going inside the house.

Nova and Leah are my two most favorite people in the world. I adore my sisters, but the tiny versions of them are a lot more fun.

The only person in the house is Nyx.

"Nova, Leah," I call out for them.

"They're on their way to Persy's house," Nyx answers.

"Seriously?"

"We have a new playroom. Mom and Dad are going to babysit them. Remember tonight's dinner?" Persy glares at me.

What is she talking about? Fuck, did I agree to do something tonight?

"Plus, you won't have an excuse to ignore us," Nyx adds.

I glare at them. "You're annoying."

Persy takes a seat and pats the couch. "Come here. We need you to help us understand why you believe Misty is the love of your life."

"Can we begin with the most obvious question?" Nyx interrupts us. "Why break up this engagement—again?"

I hate the inflection on the last word. For starters, I'm not breaking up shit. I had no idea she was back with the asshole. Then there's Liv. I have more pressing matters to fix than sitting down with these two and discussing Misty. Lastly, if they want to play who is right, I'll make her spend hours yapping about nonsense while I contradict them. Let's see who is better at this game.

My love life is my problem, not theirs.

Instead of sitting next to Persy, I choose the chair. I set my feet on top of the ottoman and look at them. "I didn't break their last engagement."

"No, but it's right when she's back to planning the wedding when you want to make your move," Persy states. "Why not before?"

"I wasn't ready. You guys fell in love and got married when your lives were steady."

Both look at each other and snort.

"As if," Nyx says.

"I had lost my job. My former employer threatened to disbar me, and I was pregnant with Edward Bryant's child when I met Nate," she pauses and gives me an eye roll before saying, "Sure, let's call it a steady life."

"So, you're not in love with her," Persy states.

"What?"

"You claim that we didn't fall in love until…" She licks her lips. "You can't set falling in love as a goal. It just happens. You think you're destined to be with Misty because she's comfortable."

"That doesn't make sense."

"It does," Nyx supports Persy's statement. "I'd believe that you're into Misty if you said you've been crazy in love with her for years, but the circumstances have made it impossible for you until now."

"That's exactly it," I claim. "I was too busy to notice her."

Which is partially true, or maybe it's not. I don't care anymore. I just won't agree with them—at all.

"No, no, no," Persy says, her voice is almost a squeak. Obviously, I'm frustrating as fuck.

She sits down straight, places her palms on her thighs, and looks at me intently.

"You can't invalidate my feelings because they don't make sense to you, Persephone." *See, I can say fancy words like a therapist. Take that, Persy.*

She arches an eyebrow and crosses her arms. "So, you love her."

"What kind of question is that?" I lower my feet to the ground and stare at them, appalled. "Of course, I do. She's one of my best friends. Who else could be as perfect as she is?"

Liv, but that's never going to happen. Listen, I know they're right in some way, but if they want to have this ridiculous intervention, I'm going to give them hell.

Persy blinks twice. "Tsk, tsk, tsk. You seriously think that's enough. She's my best friend, therefore we'll make the relationship work."

"When you're in love, you feel passionate about that person. You can't imagine your life without her. In fact, you look for an excuse to call, text, or videoconference her," Nyx explains. "Neither one of you would care if you lived in a tent down in Costa Rica or a one-bedroom apartment downtown—as long as the two of you are together."

"She's right," Persy takes over. "I could live without Ford. I just don't want to live without him. My life would be colorless, tasteless, and boring. Can you say the same about Misty?"

"How many times did you call her from Costa Rica?" Nyx fires up the next question.

I'm under siege and not in the middle of a freaking intervention. These two should work for the CIA or the FBI.

"I don't think you can compare what you feel for Ford with what Nyx feels for Nate." I look at Persy, then turn to my sister. "Love is different for everyone."

"Yes and no," Persy counters. "The butterflies in your stomach.

The heart palpitations, pulse-quickening, and blood pumping faster than the speed of light is a reaction most have when they fall madly in love. There's this person you want to call when something good happens to you. A person you want to be with when the world seems to come to an end."

"The fact that you didn't call Misty while you were away says a lot about your relationship with her," Nyx concludes. "When we're on vacations, you don't even mention her, call her, or even bring her along with you."

"While I was in Costa Rica, I thought about her," I claim, but did I really think about her? I was thinking of Liv and how she's been ignoring me since November. "Perhaps it's time that I take the next step. My company is doing well enough to support a family."

"If things between the two of you felt right, you wouldn't have doubts. You would jump head-on because you trust yourself. Your love. The future you can build with her. It's like your businesses. Not one of them worked because you didn't believe in them. This last one did because it was yours—you were passionate about it."

I rub the back of my neck, wondering if I should tell them it is something that Olivia and I came up with a long time ago. We worked hard to make it happen.

"You feel lonely," Persy concludes. "As I told you, she's comfortable, but not the person who can be your safe place. She's someone who is there for you. It feels good, but will she feel good enough to become permanent? Will she be okay if you leave her for months and you never call her? Will she join you because she can't live without you? Unless you're one hundred percent sure about your relationship with her, you should let her go. Support your best friend in her next chapter. This is about her happiness, not yours."

Chapter Thirty-Three

Olivia

I SHOULD'VE SAID no to Holly's invitation. Of all the places in Denver, I have to be in the same restaurant as Eros and his family. I am in the corner waiting for Holly to arrive—or to cancel. I should leave and text her that I can't be here. She'd understand if I tell her that Eros is in the same restaurant. The two women with him are his sisters. His fiancée is not with them. The two guys next to them look a lot alike. I assume they are Persy and Nyx's husbands. Eros told me once that they were twins.

"Why are you hiding here?" Holly asks when she spots me.

"Hi." I wave at her. "Where is Calvin?"

She points at him, as she drags me away from my hiding spot. "He's greeting our friends. Come with me."

"Holly!" Persy says animatedly.

"You know them?" I mumble.

"Persy, Nyx, let me introduce you to my best friend, Liv," Holly says. "Liv, this is Persy, Nyx, and Ford." She points at the tall guy next to Calvin. "Where is Nate?"

"With my brother," Nyx responds, pointing to the other side and then shaking my hand. "I've heard so much about you. It's nice to finally meet you."

I look at Holly. She frowns. It takes a slight glance to where Eros stands for her to understand why I am freaking out and we should leave right about now.

"Chadwick, party of eight, we're ready for you."

Holly links our arms together and says, "I'm so sorry. I had no idea."

"You don't understand, I need to leave."

"Don't let him ruin our night," she says. "I'll talk to his sisters. I thought he was single."

The last sentence slams into my chest.

"Were you trying to set me up with him?" I whisper-shout.

Is she fucking kidding me? I told her to stop setting me up.

"He sounded good until—"

"He's getting married," I argue. "How is it that his sisters are setting him up?"

We enter a private room. Great, let's make this situation more awkward than it already is. This would be a great time to have some superpowers, like invisibility or teleportation.

I know the exact moment when he sees me. His penetrating gaze sweeps my body. "Liv?"

"You two already know each other?" Nyx asks.

Eros stares at me. He's pinning me with his gaze. I can't move. It's as if he's making sure I don't disappear.

"How do you know her?" Persy asks.

"Oh, you don't know?" I extend my hand. "Olivia Sierra. I might be his wedding planner. Unless his fiancée decides I'm not good enough to buy flowers for their big day."

Okay, I could've been less sarcastic, but what the hell is wrong with him? He's organizing his wedding earlier, and now he's being set up. I thought he told everything to his sisters. Obviously, I'm not part of everything.

"You're getting married?" Nyx asks. "I thought we talked about it earlier today."

"Who are you marrying?" Persy demands.

"You don't know Misty?" I look at Persy. "*His college sweetheart.*"

"What is she talking about?" Nyx demands.

"Ladies, we only allow one intervention a month," Ford says and laughs. "Let's sit down and have dinner."

"Can we talk?" Eros tilts his head outside the room.

"I'd rather not," I answer. "Why didn't you invite *your fiancée?*"

"Why don't we sit down?" Persy suggests. Everyone moves, but I can't. My back is against the wall, and Eros is almost caging me.

His hand lifts, and I warn him. "Don't touch me."

He blows out a harsh breath. "Liv, I need you to listen to me for five minutes. I've been calling and texting you for the past four hours to give you an explanation. You keep ignoring me. Just like you've been doing for the last five months."

"I'm not working. You can make an appointment with my assistant next week."

"Fuck!" he growls. "After everything we've been through, the least you can do is give me the benefit of the doubt and five fucking minutes to explain."

"Am I missing something?" one of his sisters asks.

"Not now, Persephone," he growls.

"I thought it was weird that you stopped answering my texts, and you went AWOL on me. Now I get it. You were going to get married—to your college sweetheart. Do you understand what that makes me? What you made me?"

He scrubs his face. "Shit. You can't possibly believe that I'm with her—or that I lied to you all these years." He pauses and scrubs his face with one hand. "I. Don't. Lie."

"You can't say that when you valiantly came to me asking to organize a wedding." My tone is calm, very business-like.

"If I was getting married, I'd tell you." He raises his voice. "I tell you everything. What about you not answering my texts. I've been texting you and calling you, and you haven't answered me." He waves his phone up in the air.

"Save your explanations." I draw air quotes. "I don't give a shit about you anymore, Eros, or whatever your name is, liar."

"I fucking knew you were upset. She's not my fiancée. I swear to you, Liv. We never dated. She's marrying fucking Richard Prince. She wanted to scout the place and you before... Since when did you become a wedding planner?" He shakes his hands. "I'm... I feel like I lost a chunk of your life. Not only that, now you're banning me from it because of my friend's insecurities."

"Sorry to interrupt, but the rest of us would like to have dinner," one of his sisters interjects. I'm not sure who because Eros and I aren't breaking eye contact. "Can we have dinner, and then you can solve your issues?"

"Liv, please." His agonizing tone is breaking through my anger. "I've never lied to you. I swear. Give me just a few minutes."

"Maybe. After dinner."

The tension in his shoulders disappears. He smiles. He's about to bend to kiss me, and I stop him. "Don't," I order.

He runs a hand through his hair. "Can you at least tell me why you've been ignoring my calls and texts?"

"I haven't heard from you since mid-November," I say as I head to take a seat. When I look at the table, I realize we're sitting next to each other.

He pulls out my chair and waits for me to sit. I realize that everyone is staring at us.

The waitress smiles. "My name is Teagan. I'll be your server for the night. May I offer you something to drink?"

I notice Nyx and Persy are looking at each other. I recall Eros mentioning that a slight glance between the two of them sometimes is an entire conversation.

"Liv, Holly was telling me that you two have known each other since kindergarten," Persy breaks the awkward silence.

"Preschool," Eros corrects her. Persy arches an eyebrow.

"Did you live in San Francisco all your life, and you just moved to help with the business?"

"No, I..." I have no idea what to answer. Sure, they are nice, but I don't know them well enough to tell them the story of my life.

"Leave her alone, Persephone," Eros growls.

"It's called social interaction. You try to get to know people by asking them questions and providing answers."

"I'm aware of how that goes." He groans. "I need you to keep your inquisition away from her."

Nyx studies me. "You look familiar. I just can't remember where I met you, Liv."

"We haven't met," I answer.

"Are you sure? I feel like I've seen you before," she insists.

"Tacoma Airport," Eros answers. "The time we went to some national park in Washington state."

Persy snaps her fingers and smiles. "Airport girl."

I look at Eros. "Airport girl?"

He shrugs. "They come up with nicknames all the time. If I were you, I'd just ignore them."

"Wow, so we're not allowed to talk to her?"

"He's afraid you'll say something to Misty, his fiancée."

"Damn it, I'm not with Misty. She's nothing to me."

"Funny, because earlier we were having a totally different conversation." I snort. "You wanted to see if I was good enough to organize the wedding of your dreams—*with her*. She doesn't look like your type though."

"I know what you mean," Persy says. "We were just telling him to stay away from Misty." She pauses and glares at her brother. "But he's obsessed with her. He claims that she's the woman of his dreams."

"That puzzles me. I thought he didn't believe in *soulmates and shit*," I add to the conversation.

"He does, but he's just lonely," Persy claims, then lowers her voice. "I think someone broke his heart."

"Misty?"

She shakes her head. "Nope. After someone broke his heart, the Misty obsession began."

I frown, trying to remember if he has mentioned anyone in the past. I come up with nothing.

"*He* is here," Eros claims.

"Why her?"

Persy sets her hands on the table and leans closer to me. "He's known her for eighteen years. She was in love with him until she met her fiancé. Once he stopped having her attention, boom. All of a sudden, he's wondering if he missed his chance."

"Oh my God, it wasn't a hypothetical question. You were talking about yourself. Well, you know what I think about that."

218 CLAUDIA BURGOA

"He's an asshole?" Persy asks.

I nod.

"He's doing it to fill a void. Maybe the one, the woman of his dreams left," Nyx adds. "I agree with Persy's theory."

"It's easier to pine for an unavailable friend than to look for someone who might not choose him," Persy says, and stares at me before she continues, "Unless—"

"Stop analyzing me," he warns her. It's funny how she retreats. Almost as if she knows he's about to snap. "I knew you three should never be in the same room."

Nyx gives me a questioning look. Thankfully, Teagan is back. "Are you ready to order?"

"Would you mind giving us a couple more minutes? We have been entertained by their conversation," Nate requests.

"Can we go outside to discuss this?" He looks at me, then points at his sisters. "You know them. They're not going to let it go."

"She knows us?" Persy huffs.

I turn to look at them. They're staring at us, confused. I nod a couple of times. We leave the room. When we're out of the restaurant, Eros pulls out his phone, taps it a few times, and waits for something.

"We came outside so you could make a call?"

He shows me the phone. "I'm calling you, and you're not answering."

I take my own out of my purse and show it to him. "No one is calling me."

I show him his texts. The last one is a picture of Nova and Leah during Persy's birthday. Plus, all my unanswered texts. "You ignored me."

"That's not my number anymore." He takes my phone, taps a few keys, and then shows me my list of blocked numbers. "You fucking blocked my number. Why?"

"Who knows. You probably sent something incoherent?"

He looks at his thread, and I see there are a lot of texts. The top one says, "Hey, hottie. Text me."

"Of course I blocked that. How about, 'This is Eros, I changed my phone number'?"

He blinks a couple of times and shakes his head. "Well, here is everything you've missed for the past... almost four months."

I scan them. There are pictures of him and his nieces. Leah's second birthday. The news that Nyx is pregnant again. His planned trip. Photos from Costa Rica. Him asking why I'm ignoring him.

"Why did you change your number?"

"Remember when Nyx or Persy set me up with some woman who was too intense? After one date, she was expecting a lot from me. She wouldn't stop calling me or going to my house."

"Ariana?"

He nods. "Her stalking got out of hand."

"Why didn't you tell me?"

"You were busy," he answers. "Nyx helped me get a restraining order. I changed phones and sold my house."

"Was it that bad?"

He nods. "I was never with Misty. I wasn't with anyone for that matter. I've been honest with you, always." He's about to touch me, but I step aside. "You don't believe me."

"Maybe I do. I don't know. It's a lot to process."

"I unblocked my number and added it to your contacts." He shoves his hands in his pockets. "Why do I feel like you've put a barrier between us?"

"What do you mean?"

"You're not letting me get close to you or touch you."

I half-smile. "I'm done being your fuck buddy, Eros. The person you search for when you feel lonely. With Misty, you at least thought, well, you'll just marry her and be done with it."

As I'm heading back toward the restaurant, he catches up with me and says, "You're taking this all wrong."

"I might be younger than you, but I'm not an idiot. Eighteen-year-old me would've believed anything you said. Lucky for me, I'm older and wiser."

When we arrive at the table, I kiss Holly on the cheek. "I appreciate the invitation, but I'm leaving."

I turn to look at everyone else. "It was nice to finally meet you."

"Liv," Eros calls after me as I make my way out. "Why are you leaving? I thought—"

"I'm going to tell you what you thought. You believed that I'd never come into your world. That it was safe to have this virtual friend. The fuck buddy who you could reach out to whenever it was convenient."

I close my eyes, holding the tears. Why didn't I realize I had feelings for him? Until now, I thought it was a fling. It wasn't. I was falling and falling hard. I love him like I never loved anyone before—because it's always been him.

My one.

For years it's been just him in my life, while he was pining for his friend, going out on dates, and having a life. I'm my mother. God, she told me when he was helping us take care of her, "He's just using you, Olivia. Be smarter than me."

"Liv," he whispers.

"Lose my number," I say and walk away.

Chapter Thirty-Four

Eros

MY CHEST CONSTRICTS as Liv walks away from me. I can't breathe. My heart stops. Fuck, I want to respect her wishes, but I can't just let her go. As I take a step forward, I hear my annoying sister ordering me, "Stop."

"She's walking away," I mumble.

"Are you having trouble breathing?" Persy asks.

I don't answer, but fuck if I don't feel like I'm about to die.

222 · CLAUDIA BURGOA

"Why haven't you told us about her?" Her voice is calm, not the usual inquisitive annoying sound that drives me insane at times.

"Let it go, Persy."

"Because she's the one thing you don't want to share with anyone," she answers. "Have you ever been in love?"

"No, according to you."

"When you fall in love, you can't live without that person. The moment you see her, your face changes. You smile and there's no one in the room but her. Being apart kills you. You seek that person all the time. She's the first thought in the morning, and the last at night. When something good happens, you want to tell her first. When you feel like the world is about to end, you seek her. Seeing the person hurt is a thousand times more painful than anything you've ever experienced. Unless that person walks away from you."

I toss my hands up in the air. "What do you want from me?"

She puts a hand on my arm. "How long have you been in love with her?"

I run a hand through my hair. "It's not like..." I close my mouth, because who the fuck am I kidding? *I am* in love with Olivia.

"She broke your heart, how?" She fires another question. "Can you remember when you fell in love with her?"

"When did it happen?" I look up at the sky and take a deep breath. "I don't know. It could've been between the time I saw her in Tacoma, when I went to San Francisco, or during all those texts we exchanged. The time was never right for us. It's like she's leaving when I'm arriving, or she's arriving just as I'm about to leave. Our lives don't align, and she lives in a different state. Every time I tried to tell her to come with me, to be with me, she'd say, 'In another life.'"

"She's here," Persy whispers and kisses my cheek. "She's mad at you because her heart is broken. Gather the pieces and glue them together. I think I understand why you can't fall in love with anyone. She's your forever."

No. Liv is my everything.

I go back inside. Holly is my only hope.

"How long is Liv going to be in Colorado?" I ask her.

"Leave her alone," she orders.

"I would, but I can't. Not until she listens to me and knows how I feel about her."

Holly glares at me. "Liv needs someone who'll be by her side. Not a guy who disappears all the time. She's the rock of her family. She needs a guy to lean on, not someone who is in love with his best friend."

"Who do you think was there for her when Otto had a heart attack or when Beatriz was diagnosed with cancer?" I ask her, appalled. "Misty made sense because, as my sisters said, sometimes I feel alone. *Olivia can't settle in one place.* First it was Seattle, then, San Francisco. For the past few years, it was Boston. Today it's Colorado. Tomorrow it might be London because the new branch isn't working the way Otto wants. I don't want to be the person who holds her back because she hasn't found herself yet. I never want to be that person."

Holly smiles. "She's here for another three or four months. After that, it's up to her."

"Where can I find her?"

"If you know her well, you should know that finding her right now is not the answer. If you think you are who she needs, then you should know you're at a point where words aren't going to fix anything."

She's right. Radio silence aside, I've been putting this off for too long. Liv said it earlier, she is done being my fuck buddy. She wasn't ever in the first place, but from the outside, that's exactly what it looks like. This is the moment when I have to ask myself, is Olivia Evelyn Sierra the love of my life, or should I let her go?

The answer comes so easily. She's more than love. She's everything I always needed.

"Listen, I understand she needs time. I respect that, but I need an address, please."

She looks at me. "Promise you won't do anything stupid?"

"I swear."

She scribbles something on a napkin and hands it over to me.

"Sorry for ruining the night," I apologize to everyone and hand my credit card to Nate. "Dinner is on me. I have to go."

SINCE I CAN'T FIND any place open that sells cronuts, I buy a half dozen cupcakes, a grilled cheese sandwich, and chicken noodle soup. I park in front of her house. It's funny that she lives close to me. I leave the stuff in front of the door, knock, and leave.

Once I'm in my car, I text her.

Eros: *I'm sorry for today.*

I throw the phone in the console, start the car, and drive away. Five minutes later, I arrive home. Misty calls.

"Yeah?"

"Hey, can we talk?"

Honestly, I don't want to talk to her. She has no idea what she did today. It probably wasn't her. It was me. I've handled my life too loosely. My love life is a disaster—also my fault. My feelings toward Misty are an excuse to keep everyone away from me. Persy is right. Olivia is mine. I've been hers for a long time.

"I'm listening."

"In person," she clarifies.

I sigh. "It's been a long-ass day. Can it wait?"

"No. Can I come and see you?"

"Why don't we FaceTime?"

She mumbles something, and my phone rings, asking to Face-Time with Misty. I accept, and her face appears.

"You've been in this weird mood today. What's happening?"

"Is this why you need to talk to me?"

She shakes her head.

She sighs. "Listen, Richard and I have been talking. As I told you earlier, we're trying to patch things up."

"I'm glad, but are you sure that's what you want to do?" I ask, not because I'm interested in her.

Fuck, all it took is for Olivia to step back into my life for me to come to my senses. This is it. We're going to stop living in some alternate reality. I'll convince her that we belong together. That I need her in my life—forever. We're soulmates. The reason we met is because she's always been part of my life. Because my heart has always been hers.

"Yes. I do, because I love him."

"Then, I'm happy for you two."

"But here's the thing. He feels threatened by our friendship. I don't think we should see—"

I chuckle because I know where this is going. "You are breaking up with me."

"Not necessarily."

I smile and ask, "It's yes, but you don't want to do it. What do you want me to say?"

"I... I don't know. We've been friends for eighteen years. It's going to be hard not to have you in my life, but it makes sense. I thought that maybe someday we'd end up together. He knows it," she whispers the last three words.

"But we were meant to be *just* friends. A friend once told me that people come into your life for a reason. Maybe I came to yours so you could meet Richard."

Her eyes look watery. This is pretty messed up, but I really understand his request. "Well, I just wanted you to know why—"

"It's all good."

"Can I ask you something? Did you ever think of me as more than a friend?"

Persy and Nyx were on point too. I was feeling lonely. All because Liv was too far.

"If we had gotten together, it'd have been because we felt alone and not because of love," I respond.

"This is what I like about you, your honesty. Can you tell me about Olivia, the wedding planner?"

"What about her?"

"She's someone special to you," she states. "Isn't she?"

I nod and say, "Take care, Misty."

"You too, Eros."

Chapter Thirty-Five

Olivia

THE DOORBELL RINGS. When I check the camera, I see Eros bending over and then walking away. I wait for a couple of seconds before opening the door. A small white box and a takeout bag lay on the doorstep. I'm tempted to ignore them. I don't. I pick them up, curious about what he left. I set them on the dining table, staring at them for several minutes.

Opening them feels like I'm accepting his apology. I don't know if I want to see him ever again. But then, I miss him so much. I decide to open the bag first. There's an item wrapped in tinfoil with a post-it on top.

I'm sure this isn't as good as the ones you prepare. Have I ever told you grilled cheese sandwiches are my favorite? They remind me of you.

Eros

P.S. I'm not a big fan of chicken noodle soup, but I added it because they always go together.

The only times I've cried as an adult were when Dad had a heart attack and Mom was going through surgery and chemotherapy. Who knew that a sandwich would make me sob just as much? There are too many emotions spinning through my heart and my head. Love comes easy for me. Loving one person and not knowing what to expect is scary. Maybe it's one of the reasons why I never wanted to discuss anything serious with Eros.

So what if he doesn't love Misty? That doesn't mean much. I can't continue hoping that we'll see each other and then lose him again. Not that he's mine to lose in the first place. When I open the white box, there's an assortment of cupcakes. The note is on the lid.

I couldn't find cronuts. The best I could come up with were cupcakes. I'll drop off some cronuts tomorrow morning.

E.

P.S. It's never goodbye between us.

"Then what is it, Eros Brassard? You never stay!"

I hate to cry. These aren't sad tears. They are angry, frustrated, enraged tears. I'm confused by how I feel. Why didn't I realize that I love him? When did I give him my heart? I bet he doesn't even care about it. According to Eros, I'm still the same stupid kid he saved at the airport.

"They call me 'airport girl!'"

His stupid text means nothing to me. He's sorry? Sorry about what?

I call Holly. How dare she give him my address? It wasn't enough that I told her to stop introducing me to the entire male population in Denver. She gave *him* my address.

"I thought we were friends," I say as soon as she answers.

"Hi to you too."

"First, you're setting me up—after I told you to stop doing that. Then, you give *him* my address."

"I did?"

"Don't claim ignorance. He just made a food delivery," I argue, biting into one of the cupcakes he left.

"How do you know it wasn't Calvin? I could've asked him to bring you food."

"Holly, I love you, but right now I'm about to pack my things and leave. Unless you have a good explanation," I threaten her.

"I didn't know he was with you when your dad had a heart attack or when your mom was going through chemo," she says, instead of justifying her behavior.

I frown, walking back and forth in the kitchen, looking at the delicious sandwich that I want to eat, but I refuse to *he* bought it.

He purchased the cupcakes too, and you just ate one.

"He told you about that?"

"It came up when I told him you didn't need someone who would only be there when he needs some fun," she explains to me. "The desperate guy who begged me for your address isn't anything like the player I believed he was. I'm not judging you, but why didn't you tell me that he's been there for you?"

"It seemed pointless. Those were the times when we'd agree that things between us would never work. Nothing has changed. If anything, I realized today that I'm his fuck buddy," I explain.

It felt weird to say, hey, I had the best week of my life, but he left me—again. It's not much different from when my parents kept sending me from one place to another. Eros just appeared occasionally, and then he was gone for a long time.

"Things between us would never work," I state. "For one, he's older. He lives here. I live... everywhere."

"No offense, but you sound like a Dr. Seuss book. I understand that you feel betrayed because earlier today he was with that girl, Misty," she continues. "That's something you two have to discuss. Now, about you two belonging. I'm not sure if that's the case. Again, that's something only you and Eros can decide—together. If you ask me, it's time for you to find a home. You don't have to be jumping from one place to another to make everyone happy. Also, he's thirty-six. Only five years older than you. Do you have any other excuses?"

"He's in love with Misty."

"Liv, he's not. The guy was distraught because he feels like he's losing you. He's beside himself. If I gave him your address, it was because he earned it, not just because he's so freaking hot that I want you to tell me all about the hot makeup sex."

"I heard that," Calvin yells.

Holly laughs. "You're still my number one."

"It doesn't hurt hearing it at least ten times a day, Hol."

I laugh. "Go to your husband. You should stop worrying about me."

"Listen, I'm not saying forgive him right away, but at least give him the benefit of the doubt. Or sleep with him one last time. Have you seen his body?"

"Good night, Hol," I say, ending the call.

After hanging up, I see there's another text from Eros. It's a gif of a puppy saying sorry. I hate that he knows how to make me feel special.

Liv: *Thank you for the food.*
Eros: *Can we try this again?*
Liv: *What is THIS?*

Eros: *Us.*

Liv: *There's never been an us.*

Eros: *You can deny it, but there's always been something between us. We can't lose it.*

Liv: *I don't think it's a good idea.*

Eros: *I'm not giving up, Liv.*

Liv: *Goodbye.*

Eros: *It's never goodbye between us, Liv.*

Eros: *Never.*

I read the last two texts several times. Every time I say goodbye, he says this isn't a goodbye, but a see you around. It's like he just can't let me go. I'm confused, hurt, and even lost. What am I supposed to do with him?

In my little experience with guys, when something ends, it's over and we move on. Why is it never over with Eros?

He doesn't love me. Why did I fall in love with him? Am I my mother? I call Dad.

When he answers, I ask, "Why did you marry Mom?"

"And I was worried about this call. I thought you were calling to discuss work-related matters. That would've been easy." He chuckles. "Why are you asking that?"

"I know why you divorced. You didn't love her. Why marry her if you didn't love her?"

"I cared for her," he explains. "I tried to do the right thing for you and for her. Mainly you. In order for her to live in this country, she needed to be a resident. It was best to marry her and get her a green card. I didn't want to live away from my baby. I wanted my girl to have a family. It made sense to me."

I sigh because so far, I can't find anything in common between Mom and me. Dad's reasoning is different. Mom came back to him because she needed help with the baby, not because she loved him.

She said that to me while she was going through her treatment. "Why were you with Mom in the first place?"

"Why are we having this conversation?"

I explain to him how I have this idea of Mom having this unrequited love for him. He was with her because of the circumstances, but in love with Dan.

"Listen, I cared about your mom. Neither one of us was in love with each other, but we tried our best because we wanted you to have a family. I knew what it was to grow up with a single Mom. I didn't want that for you. When we realized that we were both miserable, we divorced. Should we have handled your custody differently? I don't know. Dan and I wanted to be part of your life. A part of me wanted to file for full custody but it wouldn't have been fair to you or your mom. If I failed you in some way for trying my best, I apologize."

"It would've been nice not to be jumping from one house to the other every year," I say. It's not a complaint. I'm over it; but to be honest, it would've been better if Mom had stayed in San Francisco until I was eighteen.

"Yes, but now you're afraid that you don't fit in one place," he concludes.

He's right. Maybe that's why every time Eros asked me to go with him, I disregarded his invitation. What if he sent me away after he got bored with me? "I live afraid that no one will ever love me," I say out loud.

"Home isn't a physical address, but with those who love you. When you were in Canada with your Mom, Dan and I missed you so much. You're our little girl. He loves you as if you are his." He almost chokes when he says the last sentence. "We tried to visit you at least five times a year to make sure you knew you were still part of us. Love is complicated. Families come in all shapes. Ours isn't conventional, but we tried our best. Will you find someone to share your life with? It's hard to find love when you're already in love with someone."

"What are you talking about?"

"Eros," he answers. "Are you afraid that you don't fit in his life, and that's why you don't let him in yours?"

"He's never wanted to be a part of my life. Just some casual visitor."

"Passing bystanders don't stay for days when your dad has a heart attack. They don't fly to Boston so they can help you during your Mom's surgery and treatments..." His voice trails. "They don't call your parents to check on them or wish them a happy birthday every year."

"He's done that?"

"I thought you knew."

"He never told me," I whisper.

Dad's right. I love Eros Brassard. But I can't go back to whatever we had. I need a lot more than texts and the occasional encounter that ends with a see you next time. It's unsustainable. Our situation feels like a repeat of my childhood. We have a good time, but then he leaves. I'm left behind suppressing my feelings because I learned well to hide them from my parents. This time, I want something permanent.

I want forever.

Will he offer it or just end things after we give it a try? Is it even worth it to give him a chance?

Chapter Thirty-Six

Eros

"MY FAVORITE GIRL IS HERE!" I say when Nyx enters my house. She's holding Nova in her arms.

"Unk Edos," she screams, extending her pudgy arms toward me.

I grab her from Nyx and fly her around the living room and the dining room.

"I'm a budefly!"

"The prettiest one," I confirm.

Once we're done flying, I blow a raspberry on her cheek, and she laughs.

"What do you think? Should we check if there are any treats in the kitchen?"

Her mischievous grin grows when she looks at her mom. This kid is so smart. She knows she can get away with anything when she's with me.

"It's too early for sweets," Nyx reminds us.

"It's never too early at Uncle Eros's place," I say in a soft, playful voice and use the same voice to ask, "Have you thought about ringing the bell before entering, Nyx Andromeda?"

"So you can fake that you're not around?" she asks. "Nope."

I give Nova one of the cookies I brought from Costa Rica. "I have a box just for you. I'll give it to your mom so she can take it home."

"You spoil her," she says, rolling her eyes.

"And she loves it." I smile at Nova, who is eating her cookie with such joy it makes me so happy.

I turn to look at my sister. "What can I do for you?"

"If I ask why you never told us about Liv?"

I tilt my head and shake it. "That's not up for discussion."

"Holly told us that you guys met when she was eighteen," she continues. "That's a long time. You took care of her and her father when he had a heart attack. Are those the times you disappeared for weeks?"

I stare at her.

"We're just trying to understand why you kept us in the dark. We tell you everything," she argues and lets out a loud breath. "She seems important to you. You love her. It's so obvious that you two care a lot about each other."

"Your point?"

"I'm here for you," she says.

"So, you're not going to tell me I'm an immature man-child?"

She shakes her head. "No. It makes sense why you wanted to be with Misty. As we said, she was comfortable. For some reason, you lost hope."

We spend the next hour talking about Liv. All the times we came across each other. How things never worked out. It was bad timing, fear, and destiny keeping us apart. I'm thankful that she doesn't ask me why I never told them about her. Persy mentioned it yesterday. Liv is mine. Us is something we've only shared between us. It's precious.

"I also think she's afraid that I'd reject her—or let her go," I conclude. "While growing up, we traveled to different countries all the time, but we were always together—as a family. Yes, we had other issues. Money, insecurities, food... but we knew we had the love of our parents."

"You think that's why Callie resented us?" Nyx deviates the conversation. "She wasn't sure that we loved her because she wasn't with us from the beginning?"

"I do." I nod.

Zack, her husband, and I have talked about our relationship with Callie. Ever since we lost my sister, he and I had become good friends. He met my parents and surprisingly likes them—a lot. He's also my client. It's strange to think that he became part of the family after we lost Callie.

He understands that we're not the bad guys in my baby sister's story. There was a lot of misinterpretation, lack of communication, and not enough time. I want to believe that if we hadn't lost her, things would've changed between us.

"We should've addressed our relationship with her years ago," I say out loud. "At least she brought Zack to our family."

Nyx gives me a sad smile. We miss Callie, but I think Nyx is the one who misses her the most.

"What are you going to do with Liv?" Nyx changes the conversation.

"I have to show her that I'm here to stay—or go wherever she goes.," I say everything that I thought about last night out loud. "You heard Holly. I have four months to convince her that I love her."

"All those women you casually dated?"

"There was no one," I confess. "You guys assumed. I never corrected you. Persy needed material for her podcast. I gave it to her."

"It feels like there's a part of you that we don't know." Her voice cracks a little. "As if I've been dealing with eighteen-year-old Eros for almost twenty years. But in reality, you're an adult who doesn't need me to look after him."

I shrug. "It makes you happy. Having you looking after me has a lot of perks." I tilt my head toward Nova. "However, it's time to let me go and concentrate all your energy on your little ones."

"You're the best brother in the world." She walks toward me and hugs me. "By the way, Nate and I need to run a few errands. Someone's birthday is getting close."

"Ha, you just buttered me up so I'd say yes, didn't you?" I tease her, cleaning some crumbs from Nova's face. "If you don't mind me taking her to run my own errands. We're visiting Liv."

"Can you bring her home at dinner time?"

"Liv or Nova?" I cock an eyebrow.

She frowns. "You want to drag that poor woman into the Brassard chaos before she says I do?"

"I've told her all about you people."

"I noticed last night." She kisses Nova's cheek. "Make sure Uncle Eros behaves, okay."

"Where's Nate?"

"He's at the house measuring the guest room. We're converting it into a nursery."

"Where are you having the baby?"

"Here, in Denver," she answers. "It'll be easier for everyone. Nova can have a slumber party with Leah while I'm in the hospital."

"We should pick up Leah and have some Sunday fun," I suggest to Nova. "It's been too long since the last time I spent a day with my favorite girls. What do you think? Should we go for Leah?"

Nova claps excitedly. "Leah!"

"OKAY, ladies, remember what I told you." Nova and Leah nod.

I ring the doorbell, pick them up, and make sure they're the ones facing the peephole. The door opens, and Liv smiles at the girls. "Well, this is a surprise. Are you a flower girl or a delivery girl?"

Nova turns to look at me. "Am buderfly."

"She's a butterfly delivering flowers," I announce.

"Oh, that makes more sense."

"Who are you?" she asks Leah, tapping her chin. "Are you Leah?"

Leah smiles and nods her head. She shows her the gift bag. "Viz are tookies. I wan one, peas?"

"Liv, these are my favorite girls, Nova and Leah. We came to visit you," I say. "Girls, say hi to Liv."

"Hi," they greet her in unison. They grin at her. These two are so adorable, no one can say no to them.

Liv stares at me and opens the door wide. "This is low, even for you."

I shrug. "You always said you wanted to meet them. Well, here's your chance."

We help them take off their winter gear. The only problem with having both of them with me is that I have to carry two diaper bags with everything that my sisters think they need.

"Now that we're settled, why don't you follow me to the kitchen," Liv says. "If we're going to have cookies, we need plates and maybe some lemonade or milk to go with them."

"Fowers need wader," Nova reminds us, grabbing the flowers from the bench where they sat while we helped them with their boots, mittens, and coats.

Liv squats and takes the flowers. "You're right. First, we have to find a vase for them. Would you like to help me?"

She grabs Nova's hand.

Leah and I head to the kitchen. I find plastic cups, grab some plates, and take the milk out of the fridge. Leah and I pour the milk carefully. Nova and Liv are arranging the flowers as they count them.

"The cookies are ready."

"Why don't you sit down while I bring something for you guys," Liv suggests. When she comes back, she gives a coloring book and a box of crayons to each one of them.

"Were you expecting them?"

She shakes her head. "No. After a few weeks working as an event planner, I learned that some clients bring their kids. I have juice, clay, crayons... everything to entertain them while we are working."

"Smart."

"It's just a little thing, but it makes it less stressful for the kids."

Liv spends time coloring with my nieces while she talks to them. Nova tells her about Brock, her dog. I show Liv pictures of Brock and Nova. Then Leah asks me to show her pictures of Simon, her kitty. Simon is an asshole, except with Leah. He adores his human so much. The cat is always taking care of her.

At lunchtime, we prepare grilled cheese sandwiches. Liv cuts apples into cubes for them to eat.

"They are adorable," she whispers as we set them in her guest room to take a nap. I put the mattress on the floor so they don't fall down. "I wish it wasn't so cold. They'd enjoy the backyard."

"Thank you for receiving us."

She looks at me. "I always wanted to meet them. They adore you. You're seriously the best uncle in the world."

"That's one of the best compliments I've received in my life," I say, shyly. "So, can we talk about us?"

Liv chews her bottom lip. "What is there to talk about, Eros? I'm leaving in a few months. You have a life. A family that loves you. I'm still—"

"Making up excuses to keep me away. It's easier to say there's nothing between us than to wait for me to reject you." I pause, taking a deep breath before I continue. "I didn't understand why you always brushed me away. When Callie died, I wanted to bring you with me because what if I died? I wanted to spend the rest of my life with you—even if it was just one breath. What if I never saw you again? I didn't want to live without you."

"I thought it was the pain talking," she mumbles.

"It was the fear of losing you forever," I confess. "That wasn't the only time that I tried to get serious with you. Listen, I understand that you don't believe in a long-distance relationship. It makes sense. Every other year you lost your mom—and you only saw Dan and Otto a few times during the year when you were in Canada. It was a lot for a kid. You might say that you got used to it, but it made you skittish about letting people into your life."

She nods once.

"Persy asked me yesterday when I fell in love with you." I swallow hard. "It's hard to pinpoint the moment when it happened. All I know is that every time I'm close to you, I feel happy. Your soulmate theory is true. You are it for me. We can keep doing this for years. Say 'until the next time,' find each other again... the cycle will never end. I always end up back with you because we're meant to be. Though, I think we need to start this fresh."

"Fresh?"

I nod. "We date. You let me show you how much you mean to me. If by the end of this trial I can't convince you, I'll accept my fate."

"Which is?"

"I'll leave without my true love for the rest of my life. Lost without my soul mate," I say, hoping that she'll accept me.

"Holly needs me for a few months," she states. "Afterwards, I'm leaving."

"We'll leave."

"I don't even know what I'm going to do next," she offers.

"We'll figure it out, together," I propose. "You helped me find myself. I don't think you're aware of everything you've done for me, Liv. I wouldn't be where I am if it wasn't for you."

She smiles. "You did all the work. I just gave you an idea."

"No. You made me want to do better, to realize my dreams. To find a dream. I want to be there for you," I volunteer. "Whatever it is, wherever it is, we'll figure it out."

"Your family is here."

"It doesn't matter. I'll go where you go, Liv. The moment you accept that we belong together, that I love you with all my heart, I will follow you around. I understand that you need to be jumping from one place to another. I don't need a house to be with the woman I love. I just need you."

She clears her tears with the back of her hand. "What if you get bored of me?"

"I don't love you because you keep me entertained. Though, you're pretty funny. I love you because you're loving, caring, and giving," I confess. "Sure, we'll have our differences. Some days you'll want to throw me out the window. I'm not an easy person—my sisters can attest to that. My family is... different. I just hope that I'll make you fall in love with me. That you love me enough to put up with my flaws."

"Why did you think about being with Misty?"

"I was lonely," I answer honestly. "You had shut me down one too many times. I wanted someone to fill the hole in my heart. The only way I felt like myself was when I was around you. You kept saying 'in another life.' I lost hope. When you stopped answering my texts, I thought you had found someone."

She looks at the floor and then back at me. "I thought the same. Seeing you with her... she said you were her college sweetheart."

"I was so mad at her. I should've stopped her." I run a hand through my hair. "I'm so sorry. Let me make this up to you."

We stare at each other for a few breaths. She breaks the silence. "Okay, we can try to start from the beginning."

"Eros." I grab her hand and shake it. "Nice to meet you."

"Olivia, but my friends call me Liv."

"Well, Liv," I say, feathering kisses on her knuckles. "Since you're my friend, we're having dinner with my family tonight."

"What?"

"My parents are leaving town after Nova's birthday party. I want you to meet them."

"That's too fast. *We just met,*" she protests.

"But it feels like I've loved you forever."

"You're just throwing lines so I will kiss you, aren't you?"

"Is it working?"

"Unk Edos!" Nova screams.

Liv grins. "It could've, but your time is up."

Chapter Thirty-Seven

Olivia

YEARS OF READING and listening to Persy Brassard should've prepared me for this moment—meeting Eros's parents.

It didn't.

When we arrive at Nyx's home, I help Eros with Leah while he takes care of Nova. He enters the lock code, and we step inside the house without ringing the bell.

Nova takes her mittens off and puts them in a box that has her name. Leah copies her. It's incredible how close these two little cousins are; they seem more like sisters. While Eros helps Nova with her jacket, I help Leah with hers. I notice there are hooks with their names.

"Do they know how to read?"

Eros shakes his head. "No, but my sisters believe that seeing their names will help them recognize them." It's adorable to see that both girls have their own places to put away their shoes, coats, and winter gear.

They're so proper until a guy—I'm not sure if it's Ford or Nate—steps closer and says, "Hey, baby."

"Daddy!" Nova screams, running toward him. He catches her up in mid-air and twirls her around.

Okay, so it's Nate.

Leah looks at Eros and says, "Whes Daddy?" She frowns. "And Mommy."

"Mom and Dad should be here soon, but here's Pappi," a man who looks like Eros but has salt and pepper hair says. He scoops Leah and hugs her. "How's my little Lei-Lei doing?"

"Pappi!" She hugs his neck.

Eros's dad looks at me and smiles. "I don't think we've been introduced before." He extends his hand. "I'm Octavio Brassard."

"Nice to meet you, sir. I'm Olivia Sierra."

I seriously have no idea how it happens, but suddenly I'm tackled with a hug. "It's so nice to meet you, Liv."

"Mom, we talked about your hugs," Eros says.

"As I said, I'm not her lawyer if anyone sues her for being so extra. I'll ignore her calls," Nyx claims.

"Let me look at you." The woman, who I assume is Edna Brassard, holds my arms and scans me. "Just like I imagined. A woman with a good heart."

"You don't know her, Mom," Nyx argues as she walks toward us. "Sorry, she doesn't have restraints."

"Mom, Dad, meet Liv," Eros finally says. "Liv, these are Octavio and Edna Brassard, my parents. You already met my annoying sister, Nyx. The guy playing with Nova and the dog is Nate. Where are Persy and Ford?"

"They'll be here soon," Nyx says.

Her mom is more specific about the answer, though. "Persy is ovulating. They're trying to have a baby." She clasps my hands. "You should try too. Wouldn't it be lovely to have three little ones at the same time?"

"Mom, please don't start," Eros complains. "I'm trying to convince her that I'm worth sticking around for. Can we at least pretend that we're normal?"

"You should just pray that they keep their clothes on, and they don't discuss s-e-x during dinner." Nyx smirks.

"There's nothing wrong with exploring our bodies or giving you tips," Edna speaks. "If you need any suggestions—"

"This is why I never brought her before," Eros claims. "You're scaring her."

I burst into laughter. I wasn't expecting this kind of welcome. They are definitely inappropriate, as Eros always said, but so funny.

Persy and Ford arrive only a few minutes later. Though Leah was happy to be with her grandfather, her world brightened when she saw her mom and dad. These girls are so lucky. They have a family that loves them so much.

Dinner is eloquent. Everyone has something to say about their week. Unfortunately, Edna has to know everything that involves her daughters—including if Persy did it right today.

"Mom, we're not discussing my personal life," she warns her. "I give weekly advice to my listeners. I'm sure I know how s-e-x works."

"All I'm saying is that after you had intercourse, you should've laid on your back with your legs up," Edna instructs her, then she looks at Ford. "Are you wearing the appropriate underwear?"

I spit my food and begin to laugh.

Persy glares at me. "You laugh now, but it'll be your turn soon, and we won't be there to defend you."

"Mom already offered her tips to pleasure her son," Nate says, drinking from his beer. "Plus, she suggested that they start trying to have a kid. You know, so there are three little spawns around the same age."

"Can we at least give her a pass for today," Eros begs.

"If you need"—Ford wipes his mouth—"I can install cameras in your bedroom. Mom will be able to watch the action and give you pointers."

Eros glares at him, then says, "Well, as much as we'd love to continue this torture, we're leaving."

"Why don't you come this week to have dinner with us?" his mom suggests. "We'd love to see you one more time before we leave town, Liv."

"That'd be lovely," I answer as Eros says, "We're going to be busy."

"Wednesday it is," his mom confirms.

He glances at me. "Don't say I didn't try to save you from them."

We don't leave until everyone hugs me. Nova asks if I can come to her birthday party next week.

"Of course she'll be there," Eros promises.

"That was..." I can't find the words to describe what just happened in that house.

"Insane?" he asks, opening the passenger door for me.

"Your family is great," I conclude.

"They can also be a handful," he insists. "But I like them enough to stick around."

As he enters the car, I say, "You adore them."

He bobs his head in confirmation.

"I could see Dan getting along with them," he says, turning on the engine. "While Otto is flustered because he doesn't know how to react to all the inappropriate comments. Beatriz and Mom will get along well."

"I can see that." I frown. "You've thought about that?"

He nods. "I want us to create a new world. A place where our families come together."

"But—"

"No." He stops me. "Let's not say anything hasty. Give me at least a week."

"Can I—" He lifts his index finger and shakes his head. "What if I want to tell you that I'm ready to give us a real try? That I love you. You're not letting me talk."

He smiles at me and sighs.

"Either way, I don't want to hear it," he claims. "We're going through this trial where I show you that we can be together. Where I sweep you off your feet and you fall in love with me."

I want to tell him that I already love him. That I've loved him for a long time. That we shouldn't waste another day.

"Listen, Liv. I want us to be sure about each other. Earlier, I told you how I feel about you, but I haven't shown it to you. For all you know, I'm desperate because it's obvious that I haven't had sex since... your mom was sick. Or maybe you're the one who wants to take advantage of me." He narrows his gaze. "We know how needy you are when I'm around."

"You wish," I tease him.

"Oh, I do," he confirms. "That's the thing. I want this to be about us getting together because we want to spend the rest of our lives as soul mates. Not because we have a chemistry that's off the charts."

"So, we're doing this?"

He nods. "What's your schedule for the week?"

"I have work to do," I remind him.

"What's your schedule?"

"Tomorrow I have to be at the office. We have a meeting with all the branches—Dad will be there. On Tuesday, I have a cake tasting, a dress fitting, and a consultation. I don't know what's on Wednesday," I answer. "How about you?"

"I have to be at the office for a couple of hours. Also, I'd love to bring you to the office. There are a few things I want to show you," he says with so much excitement.

"Still trying to convince me to work for you?"

He reaches for my hand and squeezes it. "You can't blame me for trying."

When we arrive at my house, he walks me to my door.

"Thank you for letting us visit and for coming to meet my family," he says, caressing my jaw with the back of his hand.

"It was interesting."

He leans closer and kisses my cheek. "At what time do you want me to pick you up?"

"I have to work," I remind him.

"At what time are you heading to the office?" he rephrases his question.

"At six thirty," I respond. "Are you planning on waking up early and following me around?"

"Not like a stalker, but we're spending the week together."

A part of me wants to tell him to come inside. I've missed him, but I like this idea of doing this old school.

"Good night, Liv," he places a kiss close to my ear. "I'll see you tomorrow."

Chapter Thirty-Eight

Olivia

"GOOD MORNING," Eros greets me when I open the door. He hands me a paper bag and a to-go mug.

"Poison?"

He grins. "Now, why would I be giving you poison?"

"You waited all this time to lure me close to your family so you guys can do a sacrifice," I joke, taking a sip of the tea. "No coffee?"

"No. Yerba Mate," he informs me. "Same results, without the caffeine."

"It's tasty," I declare, giving him the mug and looking in the bag. "Cronut?"

He nods. "Yep. Now, can you tell me about this sacrifice we're performing?"

"Obviously it's to keep the yetis away." I smirk.

He bursts into laughter. "I love that wild imagination of yours."

"Only child, remember?"

"No. I'm sure that's all you, Liv." He kisses my forehead. "And as much as I'd love to keep chatting about your quirky personality, we have to go. It's fucking freezing."

"Let me grab my bag," I tell him, heading to the foyer where I have everything ready. I lock up and set the alarm from my phone.

Once we're in the car, I give him the address where the branch is located.

"It's not that far from my office," he points out. "Isn't it funny that we both live in the Denver Tech Center and work in the same area too?"

"It's close to Holly's business too," I respond. "That's what made me choose this neighborhood. I don't like to drive much."

"That brings me to the biggest question." He pauses. "What made you become a wedding planner?"

"Event planner," I correct him. "Holly almost lost her baby during the first trimester. She needs to take it easy until the little creature arrives. I'm here to cover for her."

"Of course you are." He huffs. "When is it Liv's turn to do something she loves?"

"I love working with Dad," I answer. "There's something about planning a renovation, designing an entire development, or just building a house that's fulfilling. My work is to ensure that someone has a warm, well-built place to enjoy. It might be a new family, a retired couple, or someone who is living on their own for the first time. Seeing a community that we planned from scratch grow into a beautiful neighborhood is more satisfying than I ever imagined."

When we get to a stoplight, he looks at me with a big grin. "I knew you were going to find it."

"What?"

"Your passion," he explains to me. "In the beginning, I thought it would be the company you helped me set up. You loved to hear about its progress, but you weren't that invested. This is the first time I've heard you talk about something with so much passion. Now... I might have a proposition for you."

"Is it the indecent kind?"

He takes my hand and kisses the inside of my wrist. "Oh, yes. That's exactly where this is going, Ms. Sierra."

"Interesting. What do you have in mind?" I say in a very provocative way.

"Liv, don't do that. I can't handle that voice right now. I want you so much that I might just turn around, drag you to my room, and skip everything I have planned for this week."

"Promises, promises," I taunt him. "Tell me about your proposal."

I knew he was starting to build houses in Costa Rica. What I didn't know is that he wants to develop a community.

"So, you want to hire us?"

"No, I want to partner with you," he corrects as he enters the parking garage. "Do you have a place designated to you or can I choose any spot?"

"Park in the visitor area. It's too early to contact the management office and give them your car's information. The next time you come, I'll have a pass for you."

"You plan on inviting me again?" He winks at me.

"Don't be cocky, Brassard. I'm saying it because that partnership sounds like something Dad and I might want to do."

"We can discuss it after your meeting," he says as we make our way toward the elevator.

The meeting takes the usual two hours. By nine everyone is going back to their offices. Dad, who called into the meeting from San Francisco, doesn't mention anything about Eros being in the room. When it's just Eros and me, he says, "Can I access my computer from yours?"

I nod. He shows me the area where they're building the first homes, and the tentative plans they have. "We need someone with experience that will help us develop the area in a way that won't affect the ecosystem."

"What's the deadline?"

"We're focusing on those three houses for now," he explains. "I'm not going back until November. Gil is in charge of everything while I'm scouting other places to expand. Though, I'd like to have a crew ready to come with me if possible."

"Can we visit before November? We need to know what we're working with," I explain to him.

"Of course. We can go as many times as it's needed. I'm not expecting you to say yes right now. However, I hope that you guys will consider it."

"If you can give me a written proposal, I'll discuss it with Dad," I say a little too excited. This is exactly what I was looking for. I don't want to tell him yes until Dad and I know the requirements and go through the budget.

He smiles. "I'll have it for you tomorrow afternoon."

"Are you busy today?"

"I'm spending the day with you." He winks at me.

"You're in for a treat, Brassard. I'll dismiss my assistant. Lunch is at eleven."

"The woman is bossier than I remember." He pats the conference room table. "But I might get some use out of this table in the future, and I'll be the one giving orders."

"We'll see." I suck on my bottom lip and head to my office.

Chapter Thirty-Nine

Eros

THIS WEEK I've seen Liv wearing all kinds of outfits from leggings to pantsuits. Tonight, though, she looks spectacular. She's wearing a little black dress, a pair of fuck me shoes, and her hair is tied into a fancy bun with some strands curling around her neck.

"I still feel weird that you missed your weekly dinner with your family." She leans forward, setting her palms on the table. "Your parents are leaving tomorrow."

"What did we do yesterday?" I shoot her an annoyed look. She rolls her eyes. "Exactly. You had to go over to Persy's house to help set up for Nova's party. We were there at the party. We helped clean up and stayed for dinner. I think they'll be fine if I don't see them today."

She shakes her head.

We're on our first real date. I can't believe that after so many years we have never gone out on a date. Have we gone out to eat dinner together? Yes, several times. It's not the same though. There's a huge difference between taking her out to eat between shifts taking care of her parents and inviting her because I want to woo her.

This week has been different from our usual encounters. We've been weaving our schedules so we can see each other during the day. Though I'd love to get together with her at night, we're not ready for it. My lips crave hers, my body desires hers more than anything in the world. It's been so long, but I want to make sure that she knows that *us* is more than sex. Us is about family, forever, and finding home.

I need her to know that I love her in ways that I don't think are possible to love anyone else. I love her the only way one can love their soul mate—forever. It's taken too long to get to her, but knowing that she's at the end of this journey, I'll walk this path without hesitation.

"Still, I don't think it was wise to leave my parents alone with your family," she continues.

Otto arrived on Thursday to discuss the partnership with my company. Dan traveled along to visit Liv. I invited them to Nova's birthday party so they could spend some time with their daughter. My family welcomed them. I'm sure tonight's dinner is going to send them running back to San Francisco. They might forbid Liv from seeing me again, but that's fine. I think both families need to learn to get along.

"Are you saying that my family is a bunch of savages?" I arch an eyebrow. "Because I'd agree with you. They are."

"They're lovely. I'm afraid that your parents might ask inappropriate questions."

"Or give them tips on how to have better pleasure during the act," I say and wink at her.

She covers her ears with both hands. "Oh God, I'm not sure this was a good idea."

"Is Beatriz coming to visit you?"

She shakes her head. "Not for now. Maybe when it's warmer. Mom is in Belize avoiding the cold weather."

"Mom and Beatriz in one room might be like a time paradox," I joke.

"You're kidding, but that's going to be chaos."

I take her hand and kiss it. "Nothing would make me happier than having that kind of mayhem for the rest of my life."

"Eros," she whispers.

"Liv, I know it's terrifying to give away your heart. To trust that I won't be leaving you—or sending you away," I say, but stop. These are words that shouldn't be spoken just yet. There are a lot of things we have to discuss. "It's frightening for me too, but I trust you."

"To tell you the truth, when Holly asked me if I could help her, the first thing I thought was maybe Eros and I can finally be in the same place," she confesses. "But you disappeared on me. I understand it was a foolish misunderstanding that blew out of proportion last Saturday. These past months I've been wondering what I did wrong to make you disappear from my life."

"So, you came for me."

"There you go, ruining the moment."

"I'm still wondering what I have to do to make you fall madly in love with me."

She smiles. "I'm already in love with you. If you play your cards right, I can fall more and more just by being around you." She clears her throat. "Honestly, I'm sure I fell madly, irrevocably in love with you when Dad was in the hospital. You always make me feel safe. You give me strength."

"You're the love of my life," I say. "I have a confession to make. The first time I realized that you had some kind of grasp on my heart, it terrified me. It made me superbly happy that I had no idea what to do, so I ran."

She gives me a flirty look. "Maybe we should run together." She sucks her lip provocatively. "Home."

I raise my hand, signaling to the server that I need the check. We make it to my house in less than ten minutes. I'm glad I chose a place close to my office. We barely make it out of the car before my lips are on Liv's. I'm pressing her body against the garage door.

I want to wrap her legs around my body, show her how hard I am for her. Take her mouth, rip off her clothes, but I can't. Not just yet. We have to finish talking.

"Though I need you so much, we need to talk. I want to make sure that this is the beginning of forever. That we agree this is more than what we had in the past. This time, there won't be your world and mine. It'll be you and me living our lives. Together," I say, my voice is so croaky it sounds like grunts. "Us, existing in one time zone. Not through texts and serendipitous moments."

"What are you saying?" Her lips tremble.

"Marry me," I propose, bending on one knee. Tears gather in her eyes. She mumbles my name so low I can only read it on her lips, *Eros.*

"I don't have a ring, but I have my heart and my soul to give." I take both her hands. "I don't want to wait another second to spend the rest of my life with you. It's been hell not having you with me. It's because of you that I became the man I am today. You believed in me when no one did. In a way, you showed me how to love myself.

We can live anywhere in the world, or here close to our families. All I know is that I want to bind myself to you, forge a bond that will be unbreakable even after we're gone. Olivia Evelyn Sierra, would you do me the honor of becoming my wife?"

My heart stutters as I see the loving look in her eyes. I've witnessed that look, and I can't believe I never thought that she loved me before. That we loved each other the way we do. Tears stream down her cheeks, her voice cracks as she says, "I love you. I'd... Yes, I want to spend the rest of my life with you."

I stand up, bringing her mouth to mine.

"You've always made me happy," I say, kissing the back of her neck.

"Always?"

"Yes. There's something about you that's always called to me, Liv."

"So this was your plan all along?"

"It's better than sacrificing you to some volcano, don't you think? Maybe I'll just keep your first born instead." I kiss her deeper as I take her to my bedroom. We finally found each other, in this life.

In this moment.

Epilogue

Olivia

EVERY DAY and night with Eros are amazing. This though might be one of the best of my life. We spend all night in bed, making love while promising a life filled with trust, love, and a future where we grow old—together. We emerge the next day around noon. Dad has called me several times. I missed the weekly meeting. For the first time in years, I don't care.

We only wait a couple of weeks to get married. Edna and Octavio delay their trip after we give them the big news that we were going to celebrate our nuptials in two Sundays. Holly is my matron of honor. Persy and Nyx are my bridesmaids.

I finally meet Gil, who flies to us the moment Eros asks him to be his best man. Ford and Nate are his groomsmen. Nova and Leah are our flower girls. Mom is the only one who doesn't join us in person, but she calls us on her phone and witnesses the ceremony.

It's not a big wedding, only family and a few friends. Zack joins us. Since Callie's death, he's become good friends with Eros.

Our honeymoon is in Costa Rica. We spend some time in Eros's house. It's right by the beach. That's when we decide that maybe we should dispose of my birth control and wait for nature to do its thing. It might take years or just a few months to start a family. It's like everything in our life; we don't force anything. After analyzing everything that's happened since the first time we met, it's obvious that we weren't ready to be together.

We would've destroyed the most beautiful love because we were both too young and had a lot to learn. We're still learning from life and from each other. He's making me part of one of the most wonderful families in the world. A family that has taken in my parents too. Mom and Edna are best friends. After Cole, Holly's baby and our godchild, is born, we start making plans for our trip to Costa Rica. Our family has agreed to spend the holidays with us. We have a lot to do. The next two years we're going to be building a place that's going to help families while we help nature and the world too.

Life couldn't be better.

Epilogue

Eros

SIX YEARS later

"This is payback," Persy says as we watch our boys clean the walls.

"I don't know what you're talking about," I say, giving her an appalled look. "I was an angel growing up."

I watch my four-year-old sons and nephew, Kaelan, clean the walls they painted with the new markers Grandpas Dan and Otto sent in this week's care package. I love my in-laws, but they don't have to deal with the consequences of their presents. They should learn from Beatriz, who sends us cookies every month. Those are harmless and delicious.

"Like I believe it," Liv, my wife, hands me a bucket and a sponge. "These three are trouble. Edna says that they are just like you two. If we want them to finish today, you're going to have to help them."

"Why me and not her?" I point at Persy. "Her son conspired with our spawns."

Liv rests a hand on the small bump of her belly and sighs. "Persy and I are going to the living room to put our feet up and rest. We still have several months to nest."

I love that Liv is best friends with my sisters.

Persy smirks. "I told you, it's payback. You have not one, but two like you." She points at Liv's belly. "Maybe Mr. Three is going to the worst."

Liv smiles. We don't want to tell anyone yet that we're having a baby girl. Though, if she's anything like Walker or Finley, we're screwed. When we learned we were having twins, we were ecstatic. Once they learned how to crawl, we knew we were in trouble.

"Your spawn is going to be worse than mine," I complain, pointing at her bump. "Where is your husband? He should be helping us."

"So, you agree that they are a couple of monsters," Persy taunts me. "Ford took Leah to soccer practice."

"Lucky man. And yeah, maybe my sons inherited that from my sisters," I agree.

"Mommy, can I have cookies?" Walker turns around and looks at Liv, gifting her his best smile. Finley looks over his shoulder and opens his eyes wide. "Please, Mommy."

"And here's where you can see who's the weak link of this family," I mumble. Persy tries not to chuckle.

There are times when my wife can't say no to our boys. Liv goes close to them and whispers something. They both hug her tight and my heart swells. I love to see my family like this. Happy.

"Daddy, can you help us?" Walker asks with a big grin.

"I promised to make grilled cheese sandwiches for lunch. I'll give them cookies as soon as they finish cleaning the mess." Liv kisses the top of their heads.

"Let's get started then."

Persy kisses Keal's cheek and says, "next time ask for paper, buddy."

He nods. She heads toward the living room. Since the boys are busy cleaning the wall, I grab Liv by the waist and pull her to me. "You're bossy, lady."

"Tonight I can give you a big prize for helping the boys."

"Well, now we're speaking my language." I kiss her hard. "Do you know how much I love you?"

"I love you just as much." She holds my face with both hands. "Thank you for making me so happy."

"Thank you for coming into my life and giving me so much." I kiss her again, grateful that there's only one life and we're in it together.

Dear Reader,

Thank you so much for picking up a copy of Love Like Her. I am grateful to have you as my reader and if you are new to me, I hope this is the beginning of our journey together.

The Brassard family came to me when the pandemic started. They're the escape I needed for this year. I wasn't sure if I'd be writing a book for each sibling, or just for Persy and Nyx. Once I got to know Eros better, I knew the perfect book for him. One I've been plotting for a long time.

This guy isn't exactly a man child, but a guy who wanted to make everyone happy and knew how to play the system. As much as he looked as an uncaring guy, he was taking care of Liv.

The end of Against All Odds was supposed to be this story, but after meeting Zack, I can't just ignore him. His story is perfect and I hope you are ready to read about a widower, his best friend's little sister, and a single mom.

If you haven't read Persy and Ford's story and would like to follow their journey, you can grab a copy of Wrong Text, Right Love.

One last thing, if you loved Love Like Her as much as I do, please leave a review on your favorite retailer and on Bookbub. Also, please spread the word about it among your friends.

Sending all my love,
Claudia xoxo

Acknowledgments

There are two things that are super hard for me when I write a book, making sure that I don't forget anyone because it's always important to be grateful to those who hold my hand while I write my stories and publish them.

The second thing is blurbs. Which brings me to thank you to Megan Linski and Katie McGee for helping me with titles and blurbs.

Thank you so much to Kristi. My BFFL, editor, shoulder to cry, and my person. The Holly to my Olivia.

Hang Le, my longtime cover artist. She's amazing at making my books look beautiful.

Thank you to Kim who has been taking over a lot of my tasks slowly. I'm not sure what I'll do without you, therefor you can never leave me, ha!

Thank you to Nina, Kelly, and the team at Valentine's PR. They always go above and beyond to make sure that my books are out in the world.

Darlene, Karen, Melissa, Patricia, Amy, and Yolanda for always responding to my incoherent questions. Their feedback is important just like their friendship.

To all my readers, I'm so grateful for you. Thank you so much for your love, your kindness, and your support. It's because of you that I can continue doing what I do.

My amazing ARC team, girls you are an essential part of my team. Thank you for always being there for me. My Bookstagrammers, you rock!

To my Chicas! Thank you so much for your continuous support and for being there for me every day!

Thank you to all the bloggers who help me spread the word about my books. Thank you never cuts it just right, but I hope it's enough.

Thank you to my husband, my children and my family for supporting me in this journey.

Most importantly, thank you to God because he's the one who allows me to be here and who gifts me the time, the creativity, and the tools to do what I love. Thank you for all the blessings in my life.

Thank you for everything.

All my love,

Claudia xoxo

About the Author

Claudia is an award-winning, *USA Today* bestselling author. She writes alluring, thrilling stories about complicated women and the men who take their breath away. She lives in Denver, Colorado with her husband and her youngest two children. She has a sweet Bichon, Macey, who thinks she's the ruler of the house. She's only partially right. When Claudia is not writing, you can find her reading, knitting, or just hanging out with her family. At night, she likes to binge-watch shows with her equally geeky husband.

To find more about Claudia:
  website
  Sign up for her newsletter: News Letter

Also By Claudia Burgoa

The Baker's Creek Billionaire Brothers Series

Loved You Once

A Moment Like You

Defying Our Forever

Call You Mine

As We Are

June 2021

Yours to Keep

September 2021

Luna Harbor (2021/2022)

Finally You

Simply You

Truly You

Always You

Perfectly You

Madly You

Second Chance Sinners Duet

Pieces of Us

April 2021

Somehow Finding Us

May 2021

Against All Odds Series
Wrong Text, Right Love
Didn't Expect You
Love Like Her
Until Next Time

The Spearman Brothers
Maybe Later
Then He Happened
Once Upon a Holiday
Almost Perfect

My One
My One Regret
My One Despair

The Everhart Brothers

Flawed

Fervent

Found

Standalones
Us After You
Someday, Somehow
Chasing Fireflies

Something Like Hate

Until I Fall

Finding My Reason

Christmas in Kentbury

Chaotic Love Duet

Begin with You

Back to You

Unexpected Series

Uncharted

Uncut

Undefeated

Unlike Any Other

Decker the Halls

Co-writing

Holiday with You

CPSIA information can be obtained
at www.ICGtesting.com
Printed in the USA
LVHW111543200621
690709LV00005B/850

9 798712 053469